I'm not dead yet:
Cleo's journey through the Egyptian underworld.

Fanny Garstang

For all the Evelyn and Rick O'Connell fans.

The Egyptians believed that the body and soul split at time of death before being reunited. Each part of the body and soul had its own name so before you begin my version of the Book of Gates here is a helping hand to familiarise yourself with the terms:

Akh- The soul of the deceased in the next world, in the field of reeds
Ba- the human headed bird represents the mobility of the soul after death.
Ka- the divine spirit of a person. It survives the death of the body and can reside in a picture, statue or body.
Khat- the physical body.

PRESENT DAY

She had made it! She was finally here in Egypt. Finally living out a dream thanks to the 1999 classic 'The Mummy' she had seen as a teenager. Her ambition to get to Egypt had started earlier than that but the film had re-ignited her interest. For her it had started with seeing the recreation of Tutankhamun's tomb in Dorchester and then demanding to see the Egyptian Halls of the British Museum.

She knew she wouldn't be finding any fancy tombs or hidden temples like Rachel Weisz's Evelyn, but a girl could dream. Through a family friend in Germany she had managed to get into a German expedition even if her language skills were atrocious. Thankfully their English was better than her German.

They were in the first year of exploring a new location identified by satellite and LiDar that suggested a previously unknown occupation site. So far all she had been doing was cleaning and recording shards of pottery while locals shifted buckets of sand. She knew she wasn't to expect more than that considering she was only a first year student.

She swept her black curly hair off her sweaty forehead and out of her eyes with the back of her hand with a heavy sigh and stretched her back. She had known it was going to be sandy, gritty, dusty and hot but even in the shade of the shelter it was hot and every night involved a cool shower to wash the grit off her light brown body and out of her hair that she had braided in an attempt to keep her neck cool.

She was with the expedition for a month and then had two weeks to explore the country with a male friend. She hoped that she would be doing more than recording pottery shards before the month was up.

She looked up as a shout came from the German and Egyptian excavators up the hillside. The German student she was working with looked up and then at Cleo, "do we go up?"

"Come on." Cleo grabbed her wide brimmed hat and sunglasses and ducked under the tent. She needed to tell everyone at home she did something more than record pottery shards.

Her companion ran after her with two bottles of water. She had to slow as she and Cleo scrambled up the scree to where everyone was gathered. Cleo took one of the bottles before shuffling round the group to the edge of it. She couldn't see anything but she could see two German Egyptologists talking and pointing. Over their shoulder she could see the bottom of the cliff they were on where the other half of the expedition were checking out the remains of a settlement.

She turned her attention back on the hole in the slope and asked, "is it…?"
The Egyptian next to her blinked at her, not understanding her.
She sighed in frustration.

The two German Egyptologists turned to look at the crowd and waved their hands to shoo them all away, *"morgen, morgen. Bukra."*
The Egyptians muttered to themselves before picking up their tools and heading down to their half of the tent village by the Nile. Cleo lingered with her fellow student who she scrabbled to remember the name of. Imogen, that was it!

The two men carried on talking to each other and

then stopped as they realised the two young women were standing looking hopeful. One with a beard beckoned them forward, "come and see. This is what we all dream of, *ya*?"

Cleo and Imogen came round and to the edge where a wooden ladder led down into a hole. Just the top of a plastered mud brick wall could be seen. He continued, "don't get your hopes up. It will probably be empty. It won't be a king's tomb, more likely a local lord or priest. This is an unexplored place, not known to us, lost, until science and technology found it. One day we might even find your namesake's tomb." He looked pointedly at Cleo.

"Will we get into it while I am here?"

"Hopefully. You are here another two weeks?"

"Yes…. *Ya.*"

"Maybe, before you go we'll be in but we don't know what it will be like on the other side of the wall." Cleo nodded in understanding.

"Tomorrow, we clear away the rest of the rubble, carefully, and then we will be able to see if it is sealed or has been broken into. This huge project," he gestured behind them, "is going to take years and years to unlock everything. There's the town below us and an unknown number of tombs in these cliffs and why did the town develop here? Who was their patron God? Where is the temple? These are all the things to be thought about on a project of this size. You might be in the tent cleaning and recording pottery shards but they will be telling us about what was going on here. Now, let's head down before it gets dark."

Everyday Cleo and Imogen were allow ten minutes at the end of the day to see what was going on. The compacted debris was taken away and sieved through, revealing the bricked up wall but there was no seal. They thought that at some point in antiquity it had been raided.

Until the Egyptologists shone a torch through a hole they had made and then gave a few hours for any noxious fumes to escape, no one knew what they would find. They didn't know what wealth was in the town, whether there were even any artists capable of doing artwork in a tomb. The fact that it was a town that had disappeared into the sands suggested something major had happened for all its inhabitants to flee. All that now remained was their rubbish and half metre high mud walls.

Peering through the hole by torchlight Cleo wasn't sure whether to be thrilled to be on the site of a newly discovered tomb or to be disappointed that she couldn't discern much. There was the suggestion of rubble on the floor, maybe the hint of a carved or painted wall and that was it. The Egyptologist remarked, "I don't think we will be in before you go. We need to remove the wall and then put a steel door in to deter any new tomb robbers."
Cleo stepped back, "oh."

"I can send you photos." Imogen remarked as she stepped up to take her turn at the hole.

"Thank you. That would be great."

Walking back down Imogen exclaimed, "this is so exciting! Will you come back?"

"I will try. Now I've been here I want to come back. I'm hooked."

"Even the pottery shards?"

"Yes, even the pottery shards." Cleo laughed. It helped she had found one with a few hieroglyphs painted on to it. She looked at Imogen and knew she was going to miss her new friend and comrade in pottery shards. It had taken nearly two weeks for them to feel like friends, helped by their shared experience.

"You said you were going to explore Egypt after this. *Ya?*"

"*Ya.*"

"Cancel that and stay here."

"I can't. I should be going back to uni. This is all the time I have and a friend is coming to travel with me. I will be heading back up to Cairo to meet up with them. If I could stay I would."

"Would you try to come back?"

"Yes. Definitely. You?"

"*Ya.*"

She was beginning her long day back the next day but for the moment she was getting dressed in white disposable overalls and a face mask and safety glasses. She felt like she was heading into a crime scene and in some ways she was. She pulled on a pair of workman gloves and turned on her headtorch as her generous German teacher led her into the long chamber that had been someone's tomb.

This wasn't the only profound moment of the trip. Already she had experienced a partial eclipse, stood on the hillside with everyone else to watch it. That would be something she wouldn't experience again either, stood with Imogen watching the moon encroach on the sun and making the desert feel like a twilight world, the sharp shadows gone, the heat briefly dropping and the wind whipping grit around their ankles stilled. She was just going to have to decide which one was the most exciting thing to happen in her life ever!

Now, sweeping a hand torch around, she saw where plaster had fallen from the walls and lying on its side was the remains of a wooden coffin with a scrap of linen. Through his mask he said, "be careful where you walk. We'll be working our way through centimetre by centimetre once you are gone."

Cleo shuffled round the fallen plaster and paused to stare at the scene opposite further down. There were two lines of gods and goddesses surrounded by hieroglyphics which she could only assume were spells from the famous Book of the Dead. On the west wall she saw a carved frame, the false door for the Ka to travel between the Fields of Reeds and the tomb for when offerings were supposedly brought. She wondered how many families actually did return to the tombs with offerings of food and drink every year or whether what they left in the tombs after the funerary parties was all the bodies got.

She turned from the painted plaster wall, resisting the urge to touch it. She knew she would never forget this moment. She felt like Howard Carter finding Tutankhamun's tomb. It wasn't the tomb of a pharaoh or even full of gold, nor had she been the first in but still….

She found herself stumbling on something, a fallen rock, a piece of plaster, she wasn't sure, but with an exclamation of horror she saw herself heading for the false door. Her first thought was her Egyptologist career was over before it had even started…..

HOUR -1

She found herself crashing to the floor. Opening her eyes she was expecting a floor covered with debris but it was clean and dry. Slowly she lifted her eyes from the sandalled feet, up tanned legs to a linen pleated kilt. She froze at that point. She glanced left and saw a pair of sandalled feet that way and right to where she could see a line of a mix of tanned sandalled feet and bare feet. Unable to decide if she was in a dream or unconscious she slowly stood up to find three ancient Egyptian faces, straight off the walls of tombs, glaring at her.

They were silent. They didn't even acknowledge that she was wearing something different to them. Deciding she wasn't worth their attention they turned away. The two to her right returned to talking while the third pretended not to have seen her.

She removed her safety glasses and the mask so she could see more clearly. She was in a passageway. The walls on either side were lined with doorways like the false door in the tomb she had been in moments before. Between doors there were hieroglyphics and paintings of gods holding up amulets. It began to make her feel like she was in the security line at the airport. She turned to the person behind her, "where am I?"

The old woman with grey hair and a stained linen sheaf dress sniffed, "why are all new kas like this? You are in the queue to be judged."

"Queue?" Cleo didn't even think it strange that she could understand the ancient Egyptian considering she could barely speak German.

She huffed, "how else do you think they could manage all of us?"

"But it's 2024. The Egyptians were hundreds, thousands of years ago."

"We have to get past a lot of demons and if you have a skinflint of a son like I do," the woman crossed her arms, "then you won't have all the spells to get past and you are sent to the back of the line and you, you have jumped the queue so get going." She uncrossed her arms and jerked a thumb behind her.

Cleo peered round her and saw more Egyptians behind the person she was talking to. There were men and women of all ages plus children. Of the children, some were being held in the stiff clay arms of a shabti or were holding a hand of one of the servant statuettes. Older ones looked confused. She turned back to the dead woman, "I'm not meant to be here. I haven't died."

"Well, you must be if you are here."

"I need to leave."

"Well go back the way you came in." She pointed to the doorway Cleo had come through.

Why hadn't she thought of that?! Maybe she had bumped her head harder than she thought. She turned to the door carved into the wall and pushed against it with a hand but nothing happened. She tried with her shoulder. Nothing. She even tried looking for a door handle or button for all the ridiculousness of it. Nope. She felt tears welling up in her eyes as she turned back to the grumpy Ka, "I can't go through."

"But you must be a ka though your clothes do look odd."

"I haven't died. I told you that." Cleo retorted in frustration.

"Not my problem." The old woman sniffed.

"Who can I talk to? Someone must be looking after all of

you?”

“I haven’t seen anyone for a long time.”

“Which direction do they come in?”

“That way.” The old woman pointed behind Cleo, in the direction most of the kas were facing in.

“Thank you.”

Cleo began walking. She didn’t know where she was going or who she was looking for but she hoped to find someone who could help her.

The line of kas didn’t seem to end and she began to wonder how long they had been waiting as she saw some curled up sleeping in their place in the line. Others had grouped together to play Senet or knucklebones. She stopped and stared at a huge blue faience shabti. Was this the equivalent of paying someone to wait in line for a new iPhone?

“Hey! Step away from that shabti! No cutting into line.” She turned and saw a man barreling down on her, a belly hanging over the top of his pleated linen kilt and a beaded collar round his neck. She stifled a laugh for it seemed even the nobles had to wait in line.

Panting he added, “this is my position.”

Curiosity got the better of her, “how long have you been waiting?”

“No one has moved for a long time.” He said with a heavy sigh, “all I want to do is get to the Field of Reeds and see my wife again.”

“Why is no one moving? There’s not even a small shuffle forward.”

He shrugged.

“Is it…?” It was a crazy thought that came to her and she wasn’t sure whether she should voice it. Perhaps the gods had disappeared as those that had believed turned to other religions. By the looks of it not even the brief Egyptomania of the Napoleonic era and the Victorians had made a dent

in the line of waiting kas. She began to feel sorry for them.
There was no proper afterlife for them.

"Is it what?" He demanded.
Impatience and a lack of conversation seemed to be making
everyone she spoke to grumpy.

"Well… Perhaps… Your Gods have died." She carefully
said.

"Don't be foolish girl. Ra, Osiris, Isis, they are all eternal,
just like our pharaohs."

"But only if people still believe in them."

"Believe? Of course we believe."

"I'm from…" She paused to try and work it out, "five
thousand years in the future and we believe in one god,
well some of us do, and others believe in different gods."
She saw the light die from his eyes and his shoulders
slump. He whispered, "Aten?"

"I suppose." She didn't want to destroy him any further.
He looked like he might crumble into dust at any moment.
Trying to brighten him up she said, "I don't belong here
and am trying to find my way out. If I find out what's
holding the line up I'll try and sort it so you can all get to
the Field of Reeds."
He brightened, "please. These people are all a bore. We've
all told our life stories to each other so many times I don't
know my own from theirs."
She gave him a nervous smile, backed away and turned to
continue.

Her watch didn't appear to be working so she had
no idea of the time or the distance she had been travelling.
The only way she knew she wasn't just on a treadmill with
a blue screen rotating the scenery was it was starting to get
gloomier. The queue looked more nervous and wary. Some
held tight to amulets and glanced at dark doorways. They
weren't doors to tombs now.

Cleo was wary as well. She glanced into the dark

rooms. Were the demons of the Book of the Dead hiding in them? Some just had a swirling mist in them which crept out to encircle her ankles, making them chilly even in her walking boots. Others had a feast laid out which some kas had succumbed to and now lay sprawled on the table or floor more dead than alive. Others were too dark to see anything but suspicious sounds came out of them, the crunching of bones and wails of pain.

Ahead of her, in a sudden shuffle of kas she saw a clawed black hand emerge from a doorway and pull a ka in. The amulets of the others kept it from taking anyone else. She paused and waited for the line to settle before running. This was turning nightmarish. She shouted and pinched her arms, "wake up Cleo! Wake up!"

She wasn't looking, her eyes closed in the hope it would force her to wake up, and she crashed into a physical body. She staggered back and fell on her arse. She looked up and saw it turn round. The scream fell silent in her throat.

Glaring down at her was a jackal headed body. He had a pleated linen kilt on like everyone else and was holding a spear in one hand. He had a wide band of leather round his chest held in place by shoulder straps as well as leather wristbands and armlets.

Peering round him she saw a false door but this was huge as if it would open into a banqueting hall. She saw movement in the corner of her eye and the spear was levelled at her throat. He jerked it and his head up and she slowly rose.

She thought of Stargate. The head or helmet, she wasn't sure, seemed stylised with huge pointed ears and a long pointed snout. The eyes were narrow on the sides of the mask. He had long strips of fabric hanging from his ears. He cocked his head to take her in. Unsure of whether this 'Anubis' soldier was going to be a bad guy she carefully said, "umm… Hi."

Its eyes narrowed and its ears twisted backwards like a cat so it looked angry.

"Are you Anubis?"

It scoffed.

"Oh. Umm, well… I need to see Osiris." As Osiris had been brought back to life she felt sure he would be able to get her out of this living nightmare. When the guard didn't respond she went on, "well, I don't belong here. I haven't died and to be honest everyone behind me deserves to skip the Hall of Two Truths and go straight to the Field of Reeds. They've kind of been waiting in line for several millennia now. It's 2024 AD."

She glanced behind as the kas started whispering amongst themselves. They'd fallen out of line and now arced around her and the silent 'Anubis'. She turned back, "see!"

The guard growled.

"Well, who can I speak to? Do I need to prove myself? Fill out a form? Listen to you recite poetry?" She needed to get a reaction out of him.

There was a tap on her shoulder and she turned. One of the kas had stepped forward or been pushed forward. He whispered, "no one has been allowed through for a long time."

"Does he get replaced? Are there other guards that come and take their turn?"

"Use too."

She turned back to the 'Anubis', "are you bored of being on guard duty?"

She couldn't discern it all but his posture and expression changed.

"Tell me how I can find one of your fellow guards?"

His voice hoarse from lack of use he said, "no one goes through."

"Why not?"

“Apep.”

“Apep?”

The ka from behind said, “Ra must fight him every night to be born again.”

Cleo looked between the two, “has Apep taken over behind those doors? Ra still…. No, wait… it’s Aten out there isn’t it.” She had to remember her lectures on Akhenaten and Aten, “and he doesn’t need to… He’s more eternal than Ra. Okay, why is Ra not doing his job?”

Taking everyone by surprise a head with a stiff false beard popped through the huge false door, “what is all this noise? Get back in line.”

“No.” The kas behind Cleo shouted, “we want our moment before Osiris.”

“Quiet!” A body wrapped in a linen shroud joined the head, “guard, deal with this rabble.”

“No.” Cleo found her voice.

The newcomer turned and glared at her, “no?”

“No. I don’t belong here. How many more people do I have to tell? And all these kas need to be allowed through. They have waited long enough.”

The newcomer looked Cleo over and then frowned, “you don’t belong here.”

With an exaggerated sigh Cleo exclaimed, “finally.”

“Come here girl.” He beckoned her forward with a hand, the rest of the arm still inside the shroud.

Cleo didn’t hesitate. She stepped up to him. The clawed hand shot out from the shroud and grabbed her wrist. He pulled her through the door.

She was pulled down between two rows of shrouded crouched figures. Most had human heads with the false beards she recognised from statues of the pharaohs. Some had hawk masks on. She turned from staring at the crouched figures and saw ahead of her a high dais with a large set of scales on it. It was an old school set with two gold dishes held by chains from a beam. To one side of the stage was a large chair currently empty.

It hit Cleo, she was in the Hall of Two Truths, but where were the gods? Where was Thoth recording the results? Where was Osiris watching Anubis weighing the heart with Ma'at's Feather of Truth? Was she actually dead?

She was pulled up on to the dais and across to the wall which turned out to be a backdrop that you could go behind. Down a short corridor she was taken through an open doorway. They were moving too fast the whole time for her to be able to protest. They came to a stop in the room where she managed to exclaim, "I'm not dead!"

"I know. The Lord Osiris will deal with you." Beside them a gold shabti stirred. It stiffly held an empty tray, "how can I help you?"

"Where is our Lord Osiris?" The judge of the dead demanded.

"He's not here."

"I can see that you stupid shabti. They were idiots to stop sending real servants with them." The judge grumbled, "I'll have to take you to Anubis."

"Anubis not here." The gold shabti commented.

"Do you know where he is?"

"No."

"Useless piece of…" The judge turned round, swinging Cleo round with him. His grip on her arm had never loosened and he pulled her along again.

They continued down the corridor, Cleo's eyes now watering from how tight his claw like fingers were digging into her arm. They looked like mummified hands, where the skin had dried tight over the bones. They had even ripped her white overalls. Fighting back an urge to cry she said, "where are you taking me now?"

"You don't need to know."

"I don't need to know?!"

"Stop repeating me idiot. If you are here then the word is being screwed up and Ma'at is unbalanced."
Cleo scoffed at that, "don't you see the outside world? Ma'at has been unbalanced for the last few years what with Covid, Ukraine and Palestine. America let an idiot who would happily press the red button become president. I don't want to be here anymore than you want me."

"Good. We are on the same papyrus sheet."

HOUR 1

Ahead of them was a growing light and then they stepped out of the gloom on to a jetty. Moored at the jetty was a large curved reed boat sat high in the water with a high front and back. The stern curved into a lotus plant. On it was a large cabin made of reeds.

Once her eyes had adjusted to the light she realised there were two light sources. There was a twilight like light but there was a brighter light coming from the cabin. She asked, "is that Ra's boat?"

"You are not allowed to speak his name."

"So this is Ra's boat?" She persisted.

"Quiet." He shook her.

He pushed her in front of him up the plank that led onboard and over to the cabin that looked like an open sided shrine of which she had seen models of in the British Museum. Cleo had to squint at the light emitting from the open side of the cabin. The judge pushed her to her knees, "don't even think about looking at Him."

From her hands and knees Cleo slowly lifted her head and saw the body of a man with a light so bright haloing his head she couldn't see it. He wore a linen kilt edged with two bands of gold. High on his tanned arms he wore gold armlets and the same on his wrists. Around the neck was a large collar with rows of turquoise, gold, green jasper and lapis lazuli. The body was sat on a backless stool with curved armrests.

With her eyes finally adjusted to the light she realised that the head was a gold headdress in the shape of a hawk's head and it was reflecting the light radiating around it. The sharp all-seeing eyes weren't looking at her.

His attention was on the blue faience shabti tending to a wound on his arm. He pushed the stiff moving servant away, "leave off. I'll finish it."
He spotted Cleo then, "and what do we have here?"

"She's a khat not a ka." The judge stepped up.

"So, what has that got to do with me?"

"May I?" Cleo cautiously sat up and asked.
Although there were no obvious eyebrows… do hawks even have eyebrows? She felt sure Ra had raised one.

"I fell through a false door in a tomb and now I'm stuck here. Everyone keeps saying I shouldn't be here and I know that. I need to get back to 2024 and you need to tell Osiris to sort out the huge queue of kas that want to get to the Field of Reeds."

"2024? A false door?"

"Yes. It's what we call the doorways painted or carved into tombs and that is 2024 AD, after the birth of Christ which became Year zero."

"I had a suspicion we are no longer worshipped and they prefer me as Aten."

"Ma'at is imbalanced if she is here noble lord." The judge said.

"Where is Osiris?" Ra asked.

"Not here."

"You need to sail through the night and awaken Osiris and capture Apep so you can rise again as the sun and maybe I will return to my time or dimension or planet."

"You seem to be very knowledgeable."

"In my time your history," she thought that a better word than stories or myths, "is studied and still fascinates lots of people."

"That is why we haven't faded away quite so much as the gods of Mesopatamia then?"

"Possibly. Your journey through the night is known as the Book of Gates." She added, "I know you need to fight Apep to rise as the sun. Can I help? Only you or Osiris will be able to get me back."

"Well, let's get sailing then." Ra stood up and stretched.

The judge and Cleo moved out of his way as he stepped from the cabin. He said, "Cleo, come with me. Butastis get off this boat."
The judge bowed his head and shuffled back down the plank while Cleo followed the tall god to the front of his boat.

Knowing the mythology she looked over the edge and saw four gods she didn't know the names of, talking in low voices and tearing apart a flatbread to share between themselves. Ahead of them was a huge mountain which was split in half. From a distance it looked like a thin line that the eye could barely focus on so if you weren't paying attention it would look like a whole mountain.

There was a silent signal and the four gods packed away their waterskin and leftovers. They stretched before grabbing their respective thick ropes. They dug their heels in and began pulling. Cleo was thrown forward and she saw that the gods were now in ankle deep water but the boat appeared to be sitting in deeper water.

As she righted herself she sensed Ra's presence moving away from her. He said, "come, it will be a while yet and you must be hungry and thirsty."
She turned and saw in the cabin there was now a table laden with food that she recognised from tomb wall art. There was a bowl of salad, a plate of flatbreads, a large plate with a roasted wild duck on it and some honeyed figs. There was also a flagon of beer or wine. Two settings had been placed and a simple stool for Cleo found.

Even if she hadn't been feeling hungry before she was now with the smells wafting in her direction. Her stomach rumbled as she followed him into the cabin. He chuckled, "how long have you been with us?"

"I have no idea."

He gestured at the table, "don't let me stop you."

"Thank you sir." She sat down.

As she ate, she watched the boat draw closer to the mountain and the gap within it. On either side of the opening was a kneeling bearded god, heads bowed and holding banners. One banner had a jackal's head on it and the other had a curly horned ram head. They fluttered on a breeze coming from the opening where a pivot door swung open. Inside, acting as doorkeeper, was a baboon who lit an oil filled channel in what turned out to be a tunnel. The flickering flames gave the boat a dark shadow on the opposite side of the tunnel. The baboon grunted an acknowledgement of the boat and once it had passed by the animal leapt across the channel to close the door.

Cleo was grateful for Ra's glow. She had stopped eating now, her appetite gone. She wished she was more knowledgeable of the mythology surrounding the Book of Gates so she knew what was coming. She glanced at Ra who seemed to be so still that she thought he had turned into a statue. One hand rested on the table. He had no expression on his hawk face.

HOUR 2

A bright light shaped the exit of the passage and the boat slipped through. The light reminded Cleo of those photos of soft sunlight on some piece of nature. She stood up as she realised it was like she was in ancient Egypt, sailing on the Nile. She would never be able to tell anyone what she could see and advance knowledge of ancient Egypt. She realised also she had no sense of time. She felt sure she should be tired but she felt wide awake.

She stepped out of the cabin and up to the edge of the boat. Beyond the papyrus reedbeds were fields and houses. Stiff limbed shabtis worked the fields and drew the water up from the canals alongside what Cleo could only guess akhs who had arrived with no shabtis.

It would look idyllic if it wasn't for the black smoke. Cleo turned to the cabin, "umm, Ra, is that meant to be here?"

He was already stepping out of the cabin. He joined her, "no. We will have to disembark and see what is going on. There should be the dead crowding the banks trying to catch a glimpse of me."

The fertile land of Wernes began to look charred and then black where it had been destroyed. Cleo and Ra stood in silence and the only sound was the splashes from the gods pulling the boat until the wailing could be heard.

The boat pulled up to the bank. The air was thick with smoke and the light was gloomy now apart from around Ra. Cleo hesitated to follow him but she decided it was safer to be near him then left on his barque on her own.

She ran down the plank and instantly felt the heat through her boots.

The breeze changed direction by the slightest of hand movements from Ra and it blew the smoke away revealing the ruins of a village and the dead. The akhs had died twice over. A few surviving akhs were crouched down amongst the dead while others tended to the wounded. Ra quietly remarked, "some have been lost."

"How could they die again?"
Before Ra could answer Anubis appeared at their side. The black jackal headed Anubis gave them a nod before walking off with a dark grey Set animal at his side. Cleo stared at the creature. It made her think of a small greyhound if it wasn't for the two tonged forked tail and the long anteater nose. She wondered if it would chase a ball if one was thrown.

Anubis quietly strolled through the akhs and with his sceptre pointed at those who had suffocated in the flames and smoke. The set animal bent its head to each one and as its nose touched the prone akh it disappeared.

Now the dead akhs were being dealt with those that were unharmed realised that they were in the presence of Ra. They ran towards him, wailing and throwing themselves at his feet. He held up a hand and they fell silent. He asked, "what happened here?"
A goddess with an ash stained linen dress stood, "oh Noble Lord of…"
He waved away her need to speak his titles.

"Sire, Apep swept through. The world is going to end."
An akh stepped forward before the goddess could speak again with all the long titles of Ra, "he took many of us with him. They turned to ash when he touched them. They are gone forever."

"Yes, they are sadly gone forever." Ra quietly remarked, looking over the akh's head rather than at it. He went on, "this will not be repeated, I promise you. And the world is not going to end. Your loved ones will not be joining you before their appointed time."

"What is that khat doing here then?!" The goddess demanded having noticed Cleo and still recovering from being shut down by Ra.

"She is not something to be concerned about."

Cleo stared up at Ra in disbelief that he hadn't even credited her as a person. She opened her mouth to protest and then decided it was safer to be an observer for the moment. How was she going to explain all of this when she got out of this madness?

Ra was already heading back to his barque and she wondered if he was always so aloof. With one final look around she hurried after him. Catching up with him she asked, "why has it not affected everywhere?"

"Apep is chaos and confusion is chaos of the mind." He said emotionlessly.

"What's that supposed to mean? Can you not reset it?"

"That is not for me to do."

"But you are the supreme god." She protested.

"This is not my realm."

Cleo frowned at Ra's answers then a thought came to her, "those that have gone gone, is it because their bodies have been disturbed? Is Apep the real world compared to this…" She wasn't sure how to describe the idyll they were leaving, even with its scorched village.

He cocked his head as if he was thinking, "that is an interesting thought. You should talk with my son, he understands more of both the living world and this world."

"Osiris?"

"Yes. Now, join me in the cabin as this next passage has spikes and I don't want your blood on my barque."

"Spikes?!" She turned in the direction the barque was going in and saw two pylons, two large walls that normally marked the entrance to a temple, with a passage through them.

HOUR 3

Once through the spiked passage they crossed an ink black river of water. Cleo peered into it and was surprised to find the barque floating above the queue of kas she had been with earlier.

She felt the boat sway as if in rapids and with no rudder it wanted to spin. It was disconcerting with the darkness surrounding them. The only light came from Ra and even when he stepped out of the cabin it didn't soften the dark. It felt like it made the dark darker and Cleo took a step closer to Ra.

She jumped at the sound of a loud splash and saw the black scales of a snake at the edge of Ra's ambient light. She didn't consider herself easily scared and she and her friends had even laughed at the obscurity of a snake breaking up a boat like in anaconda but now… Somewhere out there was a snake that was large enough to swallow the barque they were on.

"Apep." Ra hissed, a fist clenched.

"When do others join us?"

"Ahead are shrines where other immortals shelter."

A light from an unknown source began to give shape to the landscape ahead of them as the boat was pulled from the all-consuming darkness. Steam rose up from a lagoon of boiling water. A small overflow fed the river and steam rose from it where they met. In the lagoon was an island with two stone shrines with flaking gold leaf on them. They were narrow buildings with shutter doors and a flat roof that overhung the walls with images of whatever god was enclosed within. Cleo was too far away to discern who.

By the stream in a row were twelve more shrines that made Cleo think of a row of portaloos at a festival except some were now a heap of rubble and their linen wrapped occupants lay broken amongst the stone like most mummies were found in their tombs. Before the row was the body of a snake, its head torn off and blood dripping to form a pool between the two parts.

"Pull in." Ra ordered.

Cleo followed Ra off the barque, glancing back, expecting to see a snake rear up and wrap itself around the boat. She already thought she would be having nightmares for a while after this if she didn't die in this weird place.

She stayed close as Ra crouched before the first ruined shrine. She saw his golden aura flicker and fade. In a blink of an eye he was no longer a human body with an exaggerated hawk's head but a man wearing a cloth headdress in the shape of a hawk. A gold curved beak was low over his forehead as if it was a mask pushed off his face.

What had been hidden under the headdress wasn't a young face like she thought it would be. It was more middle aged and had lived a hard life in the outdoors. He slowly stood and said, "as you are here, make yourself useful. Go open the doors of the other shrines. Open them wide so I may awaken them."

"Are those ones dead?"

"For tonight. For tomorrow night I won't know until then. Now hurry. I can only wake them the once."

Cleo hurried to the first untouched shrine and realised it hadn't escaped completely unscathed. One corner was pushed in like a truck had reversed into it but the culprit had left a large scale caught in a joint of the stonework. It was hard to open the first half of the door due to the now warped frame but the other side was easier.

She stared at the mummy inside, arms crossed across its chest. She tried to remember what that meant. Kings had their arms crossed over their chest to mark them out for kingship while their queens had theirs held in place at their sides. A death mask covered the face but as if sensing the doors open and light coming in the bandage wrapped arms moved and pushed the death mask up revealing the feminine face of a goddess that she had no idea of which surprised Cleo. Was this perhaps the king-queen Hatshepsut. The goddess queen blinked and frowned at Cleo in her clothes that she didn't recognise.

"Hurry." Ra called out

"Yes, sorry…." Cleo wanted to ask the goddess who she was but remembered Ra had given her a task to do.

She hurried through her work, waiting for them to wake up before moving on. Each shrine held a mummified god or goddess. She called out from the end of the row, "done."

"Thank you. Now, to the boat, cover your eyes tight and do not open them for I could blind you."

Cleo didn't need to be told twice. She hid in the cabin, crouched in a corner, her back to the outside world and hands over her closed eyes. She felt the power of the God, the heat of the sun on her back and even with her eyes twice covered she still had sunspots dancing behind her eyelids. With a brilliant flash the light disappeared. Slowly she uncurled herself and took her hands off her eyes and opened them one by one.

She left the cabin and saw Ra on one knee panting heavily. She ran to him and then hesitated. Could she touch a god? What would happen if she did? Since he was the sun would she burst into flames? He looked up and she saw his face had aged even more. Was his aging happening too quickly? She knew he would grow old but they were only three hours into the night!

There was movement from the shrines and Cleo looked over to see the mummies had become more human. She recognised Isis from her red linen sheath dress held in place by two wide shoulder straps. Over the goddess' shoulders was a fine shawl that was beaded to suggest rows of feathers that if she lifted her arms would look like wings. On her head with a red hairband wrapped through her black hair, was a headdress that looked like a chair.

Isis spotted Ra and hurried over calling out to the others emerging from their shrines, "find Osiris. This is the worst I've seen him in a while." She crouched down beside Ra, her wing shawl spreading around her like a bird of prey sheltering its kill after landing, "what happened here?" She pulled him up, supporting him as Nephthys brought a padded stool. The others gathered in a loose arc round the two goddesses, Ra and Cleo.

There was a cough and everyone turned. Behind them stood Osiris in a long sleeved linen gown with a red dyed leather belt wrapped round his waist. His skin was a greyish green and in one hand he carried his crook and flail. As he stepped into the inner circle wheat grew where he had lifted his foot. Out of the shadows, following him at a respectable distance were kas who needed his blessed touch to heal them or make them young enough to enjoy the Wernes. They hung back, a silent pale group.

As Osiris passed Isis both reached out with a hand, the fingers curled together for a moment. Their eyes caught each other's and Isis let out a long sigh. He gave his wife a faint smile. One day they would be together again, forever, but until then they would have to survive on touches and glances.

With a heavy sigh of his own Osiris turned to the

Creator and with his lips pressed in a grim straight line, "what has happened to you?"

"Where is your brother?" Ra looked up from under his eyebrows, his head still hanging low.
Osiris shrugged since he didn't particularly care. He was still bitter over what Set had done to him while he was King of Egypt as well as the embarrassment of falling for his brother's trick. Declining to answer he said, "I am more concerned for you. You currently don't look like you'll make it to your rebirth."

"Do what you need to do." Ra spat out. He was too tired to care. Ma'at was unbalanced, the world no longer worshipped him but still he sailed in his solar barque, the Mandjet, with the scarab beetle pushing it along. Perhaps he could just sink back into the waters and let Aten continue being the blessed one.
Ignoring Ra's grumpy tone Osiris asked again, "what happened here?"

"Apep." Cleo answered.

The immortals all turned and stared at her. They began to frown and Osiris raised an eyebrow, "who are you khat? How have you slipped past my gatekeepers and Anubis?"

"I'm Cleo." She replied, standing straight. She wasn't going to let the staring gods and goddesses scare her, "apparently you weren't in your office, so I somehow ended up with Ra."

"Leave her be. She's under my care and I expect all of you to look after her as well. She ended up here because Ma'at is out of balance everywhere."

"This feels like Set." Isis said, "he's meant to be watching over Apep. Why do we keep letting him have important roles? If he's not watching Apep, where is he?" She glanced round the group, "where is Horus?"
Ra reached out and touched her arm and she instantly

calmed. He said, "we will find out soon enough." He looked over to Osiris, "do what you need to do as we must get on and you have others waiting for your attention." He gestured to the group of waiting kas.

"Yes sir." Osiris bowed his head and handed his crook and flail to his wife. He put both hands on Ra's shoulders and Ra's skin began to glow.

Ra lifted his head and there was a brightness in his eyes again. He put a wrinkled hand on one of Osiris, "enough, thank you. Now, go and have a few minutes with your wife. Cleo, help me to my barque."

"I will." Nephthys stepped up. She glared at Cleo, warning her off.

Isis ran into Osiris' arms while the minor gods who had been woken, the Shennu, gathered the hovering kas together to be taken care of by Osiris when he was ready. They offered the kas bread and barley beer while one looked after the shrines' serpent companion.

Osiris knew he could leave them to look after the kas for the moment. He needed this time with his wife/sister. One day they would be together permanently but for now they had to take these snatched moments. He ran a slender hand over her cheek before lifting her head so she could kiss her prefect lips.

In response she pressed her whole body against his so he would have a memory of her till the next time. He murmured, "please be careful out there. With that khat present the world is badly out of balance."

"Is she trapped here?"

"I don't know. We'll see what happens at dawn. She can not be judged as she is not a ka."

"I'd best go." She took a reluctant step backwards. He sighed and didn't stop her running to the barque just as

the pulling gods pulled the ropes taunt.
She turned and looked back and blew him a kiss making
him smile.

He wished she could stay permanently with him
then light would come back. He only had memories to keep
him going. He wanted to laugh again and dance and wear
the biggest smile like when he and Isis ruled Egypt. The
light that appeared when Isis was near slipped away with
the barque and he became somber again. His skin that had
been pink with Isis close to him was turning greyish green
again. Behind him a shennu was harvesting the now ripe
wheat, a scythe in his hand.

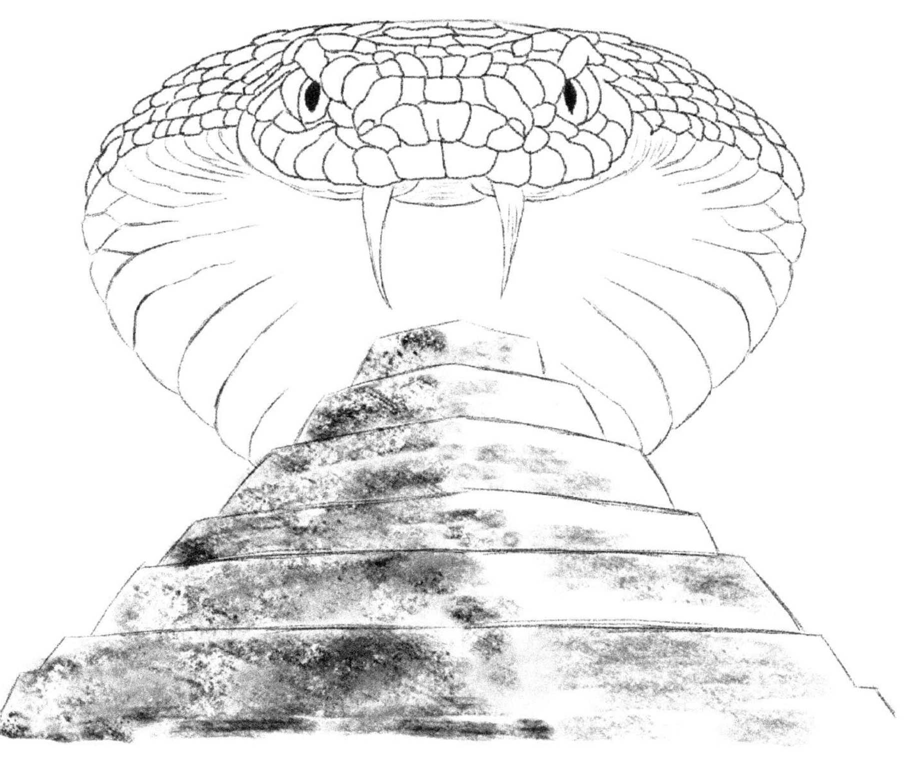

HOUR 4:

Cleo was joined at the prow of the ship by several of the immortals as the boat was pulled along into some fog that hid the entrance to another dark cavern. As they got closer she could see two roughhewn pylons marking the start of the next hour of the night.

Beyond the pylons she could see flickering low flames, but she wasn't paying attention to what was ahead. Instead she was looking at the immortals around her. Thoth with ink-stained fingers clutching at the edge of the barque wore an eye mask which had the long curved beak of the ibis on it. It made her think of a medieval plague mask but not so dark and heavy.

To her other side was Nephthys in the same style dress as her sister and upon her raven black shoulder length wig edged in golden beads, was what looked to Cleo like an upside-down top hat. The goddess kept giving her glowering looks.

Cleo was interrupted from the study of the two immortals by Thoth saying quietly, "can you feel it?"

"Of course I can feel it." Nephthys spat, "we always feel it but it's worse tonight and I bet she's to blame." She glared at Cleo and then stalked away.

"Don't mind her." Thoth commented as he looked down at Cleo, "can you feel it?"

"Feel what?" There was a tightness to her chest but she wasn't sure whether it was from the unknown destination or the company.

"Trepidation."

"Yeah." She replied unconvincingly.

"It is going to be a long night. No one knows what is going to happen since you are here and shouldn't be."

"I know I shouldn't be here."

"It's not your fault. This is Apep's doing. He is the master of chaos."

"So he brought me here?"

"Maybe." Thoth replied thoughtful, "how did you get here?"

"I was in a tomb…."

"You are a tomb robber?!"

"No, no." She hastily reassured him, "I come from a different time."
He frowned.

"In the future you are all known of but are no longer worshipped but the world is fascinated with the centuries when you were."

"Interesting. Go on."

"Anyway, I was looking at the artwork and then tripped or stumbled in the tomb and crashed through the false door."

"False door?"

"It's what we call the door that is painted or carved into the wall so that the kas can pass back and forth between the tomb and the Field of Reeds."

"You have an understanding of our world." He sounded surprised.

"You have been studied for a long time. Like I know you are the god of scribes." She gestured at his ink-stained fingers, "and you are very clever."
Thoth chuckled, "you have me there. You are much like your namesake."

"No I'm not. She could speak Egyptian and I can't. I can barely speak German even though I have been working with them."

"Well Isis knew her best. Now, I think we need to change your clothes to something more suitable." He gestured at her body in a motion that made her think of Queer Eye.

She looked down at herself. She was still wearing the white disposable overalls, now torn in places, over her t-shirt and cargo shorts. She didn't even want to know what her hair was looking like.

"I think your namesake would be disappointed in how you look." He clicked his fingers as he instructed, "turn slowly on the spot."

"Why?"

"No questions, do as I say."

Cleo sighed and decided it was best to appease the god. She didn't need an angry god especially as he was being generous with his time. Slowly she tuned on the spot, arms stiffly out as if she was wearing an outfit her mother picked out for her but she hated.

She felt a tingling sensation, a warmth rose from her hiking boots upwards until with a ping it stretched a hair upwards, pulling her taller.

She nervously opened one eye and looked down at herself. She wore leather sandals and noted her chipped nail polish was no longer chipped. The linen sheath dress she wore was made of the finest linen and was cinched in at the waist and thankfully was more modest than it looked in artwork. Round her neck was a twice looped strand of multicoloured beads and her hair had been braided to look like a wig with gold beads at the end of each braid. She wore an armlet tight on her upper arm and several gold bangles on her wrist.

Before she could stop herself she found herself posing, arm in the air, hip sticking out as she grinned, "Cleopatra, coming 'atcha."
She slapped a hand over her mouth in horror at hearing her childhood catchphrase coming out of her mouth.

Thoth was trying to hold back his own mirth at her reaction. He shook his head and took a deep breath to compose himself before saying, "now you look like you belong and no one will question it. You look like you deserve to be at Ra's side."

"Thank you… I think." Cleo blushed.

"Now," he became serious, "if you didn't believe in magic before you soon will."

"What do you mean?" Cleo looked round nervously. She realised that the flames of the tunnel were now red glowing coals. The darkness was creeping in again apart from Ra's glow in the cabin. Looking at the cabin Cleo asked, "does he really die or is it trickery?"

"He really dies."

Before she could ask another question she was thrown forward as the barque ran aground but Thoth grabbed her arm and pulled her towards him.

The barque began to creak and groan as the reed bundles started to change shape. Cleo stared in disbelief and horror as the planks of wood under her feet changed into the scales of a snake. The bow stretched upwards and split into two snake heads, tongues flickering in and out, tasting the air. Behind her the cabin was still there, perched on the flattened back of the fat snake.

Thoth let go of her as he remarked, "we travel by snake now. Look ahead, can you see a faint glow?" He pointed ahead and the two heads of the snake separated so he and Cleo could see through.

"What's out there?"

"Tem. He supports Set in guarding Apep but we know that isn't the case tonight. Be on your guard, there could be anything out there. We won't be safe until we reached Sokar's palace."

"Isis is worried about Set. Do you know where he is?" Thoth shook his head, "he is a disorder himself, just like

Apep. He will either be in league with Apep or is lying injured somewhere."

Cleo turned away and looked out on the barren landscape. She hoped Thoth couldn't sense her fear. She knew the story of how Set had tricked his brother and then fought his nephew for the throne. He was always portrayed as the bad guy and if this was a movie he would be the evil mastermind with Apep as his fluffy white cat. What would Ra be?

The double headed snake slithered along the dry ground, it's four eyes glowing into the darkness. Even though it was dark it seemed to know where it was going, slithering through streams that began from nowhere and disappeared back into the ground. It slowed down as it reached a deep curved trench and one of its heads turned to look at Thoth.

Thoth ordered Cleo, "stay there," before jumping from the snake. He knelt down at the edge of the trench and touched the ground. Cleo watched as he looked left then right and then returned to the snake. He held out a hand and the snake's two heads came down as if they were horses looking for their noses to be rubbed. In a language Cleo couldn't understand he said, *"he's long gone, keep going."* The snakes let out a long hiss as if protesting.

"He's not here. He's else where but they will find him. We must keep going and find Tem. He will have answers. Follow the trench." He pointed up the trench.
They hissed again but did as they were told and turned to follow the trench to its source. Thoth leapt back on.

Isis and Nephthys emerged from Ra's cabin and joined Cleo and Thoth as a glow in the distance grew brighter. They held tight to each other's hand in fear of what may or may not happen. Though nights like these were rare occurrences it didn't make it any easier. A night like this left them fearing the end would actually happen. For a long time they had feared that end as those who had worshipped them disappeared and they had battled with Apep most nights but then they had grown stronger again.

They glanced over at the khat and wondered if she was actually part of the chaos or something else. It didn't help that Set and the Eye of Ra were both missing. Would she even be of any help like her namesake had been? Not that even Cleopatra VII Thea Philopator, **the** Cleopatra of Mark Anthony fame, had been able to compare herself to Hatshepsut.

The snake slithered to a stop at a depression in the ground as if something heavy had lain there. In the middle of the spiral was a man sprawled on the ground with a bleeding head wound. Beside him was the end of a chain, the last link snapped open. The spiral indentation grew deeper as Apep had unwound and then headed into the silent desolate lands.

Ra stepped out of his cabin and led everyone down from the snake as it hissed nervously. It could sense Apep's strength and power to bring chaos and wanted to be away. Standing closest to the snake Cleo reached out and patted the neck of the closest head. It leant into her hand taking Cleo by surprise.

By the edge of the spiral indentation Ra stood surveying the space and the old man huddled int the centre. He ordered, "bring Tem to me."
Isis ran over and helped the man up. He began to weep as he was led to Ra. He cried, tears running into wrinkles that reflected the land they were in, "he was too strong, too strong…."
"Who did this? Who helped him?" Isis asked, trying to

keep her tone soft and reassuring when all she wanted to
know was if her son was going to be safe.

"I couldn't see, they kept themselves in the shadows."

"We need the Eye of Ra." Nephthys exclaimed from Ra's
side, "we must protect Ra even more than ever. How dare
she not show herself."

"Ssh sister, she will be out there." Isis tried to soothe her
sister.

Thoth interrupted, "the Eye is already out there hunting
Apep."

They all turned on him and Nephthys demanded, "why did
you not speak of this earlier?"

"You didn't need to know. She is good at what she does."
Thoth replied in a similar soothing tone as Isis as if he was
used to placating angry immortals. He was the one often
sent out to calm and bring back an angry Hathor when she
was rampaging round the desert in her lioness form.

"Sekhmet should have stopped her. She is meant to be
kept safe as well. We can't go to Sokar empty handed." Isis
exclaimed.

In the background as the forgotten silent observer
Cleo racked her brain to remember who or what the Eye of
Ra was. All she could remember was that the Eye was the
feminine version of Ra and his daughter at the same time
who either appeared as a feline or a cobra to act as
bodyguard to the Sun God. Basically any goddess who had
a feline form could be the Eye but most often it was Hathor
or Sekhmet.

She was brought back to her surreal present by Ra
who was staring off into the distance as he remarked, "she
will appear when she is needed." He turned to where Isis
held Tem, "Tem, come to me."

The old man took a few steps forward and fell to his knees
before the God. Ra put a hand on Tem's shoulder and the
old man began to fade and be re-absorbed back into Ra

until the Sungod's rebirth and he would return to act as jailer once again to Apep in this hour of the night. Ra's glow grew brighter for a moment as he re-absorbed a part of himself before fading again. He turned to look at everyone present, "we must go on."

Back on the snake the journey felt endless, not helped by the darkness around them. It left Cleo craving light, any light, even starlight. She would have joined Ra in his cabin but Nephthys had stopped her, thrusting one hand out and up into her face. She had spat, "you don't deserve to be near him."

Cleo didn't consider herself afraid of the dark but now she wasn't so sure. She felt suffocated by the darkness and there was the fear of the unknown. Would she survive this night? Would she get eaten by Apep?

It was with relief that she saw it begin to lighten, light highlighting a rising cliff that made her think of the high cliffs that held the wadis now more famously known as the Valley of the Kings and Queens. The cliff face was dotted with the sealed doors of tombs. Others stood out in the terracing with shrines which then led down into the ground. Dominating the lightening skyline was a step pyramid like the one at Saqqara Cleo had been planning to see.

The snake came to a stop at the bottom of the cliff where a processional way lined with carved ram headed sphinxes led up to the pyramid. It went straight up the cliff, a long shallow ramp, ignoring the height of the rockface, to a mortuary temple that was in front of the step pyramid.

The group began the long walk up the ramp. As they passed each sphinx it would bow its head in acknowledgement to Ra. The paved path ended at the colonnaded entrance of a mortuary temple. Before her was a long row of pillars faced with statues representing Osiris in his dead form, arms crossed with the flail and crook. Behind the row of pillars was a large wall with a small, in comparison, doorway leading into the temple. The names of the dead were written in hieroglyphics. It reminded Cleo of the old style train information boards which would click through as a train departed but this one was frozen half changed as the last ka had passed through the Hall of Two Truths and the names would have moved up the list. If she got out of this she knew she would need to give some offering to these ancient gods so the kas could finally stop waiting.

She turned away from the list to the presence in the doorway. Standing there, hands clasped behind his back, was a falcon headed man with grey green skin. His keen eye cast over them all and lingered on Cleo a moment longer than the others, his head cocked.

He turned back to the others, "welcome back."

"It is good to see Apep hasn't touched here." Thoth commented.

Sokar frowned, "of course he hasn't. Tem is keeping watch over him is he not?"

Thoth shook his head.

"Oh? I wondered what that rumbling was earlier. And where is my charge?"

"Out stalking Apep."

"Oh." Sokar hid his relief as depending upon Hathor's mood she would either be good company or a nightmare, throwing a tantrum like a spoilt child. It had been known to take a tomb's worth of shabtis to bring her under control when she was in a foul mood. He went on, "I'm sure you'll be able to imprison him again and who is this?" He turned to look at Cleo, "she's not a lost soul. Come here girl."

Cleo stepped closer.

Sokar lifted her head by her chin and studied her face, "interesting, very interesting. Ma'at will not like this. What is happening in the outside world?"

"Apep." Cleo carefully replied. She decided that he would understand that more than the politics of her century.

"Mmm… you think me unintelligent. We may live here but I know of the khat world. I am aware of the wars and the plagues. I know that your world is in flux. Without your world still revering us we wouldn't be alive."

"What about the kas waiting for their fate?" She found her voice, "you are a god of the dead, why have you not looked to them if Osiris has not?"

"Enough." Ra interrupted.

"We must talk later, you and I." Sokar chuckled, "you'll be keeping me and Ra company anyway. I can't give all my secrets away. What lies ahead in my palace for my immortal brethren you would not survive."

"Are you sure I should?" Cleo asked nervously. She wasn't sure she deserved to witness the embalming of Ra.

"Yes. You can not perish here, Apep would win." Ra remarked.

"You think I was brought here by Apep to test you or something?"

"I am a creation, not the creator. I don't understand it all myself."

"Ra, it is time." Sokar put a hand on the Sun God's arm.

"Yes of course."

Cleo followed the two gods through the mortuary temple leaving the others behind. The further in they went the more like a tomb it felt. The walls of the corridor were painted with moving images of kas and shabtis working the black silt fields of the Wernes. Others showed kas relaxing with musicians, dancers or having a meal with family. They passed through a stone cut antechamber supported by squared off pillars. The walls were blank but the pillars held larger than life images of the gods. In the next corridor the images moved once again as kas knelt before the gods, offered goods to the gods and prayed their hearts were pure enough against the Feather of Truth.

She had no sense of whether they were going up or down or were still on the level as they walked and then finally entered a room where there was a large block of granite with a blanket draped over its centre. She felt sure this was the centre of the mortuary temple. A few torches flickered revealing blank walls but otherwise they were shrouded in shadows.

She lingered on the threshold as Sokar put a hand to Ra's forehead. The light Ra admitted faded like a fire that had burnt through the last of its wood. As Ra sagged Anubis stepped out of the shadows and caught the Sun god in his arms. The torches round the wall flickered to almost going out as if to acknowledge the death of the god.

Anubis was as silent as the first time she had seen him and he acted with great tenderness as he lay the body on the stone slab. From out of nowhere he pulled out a rolled up cloth toolkit holding knives, scoops and hooks for removing the body's organs. She watched Anubis calmly cut into the left side of the body and remove all the organs apart from the heart and put them in four canopic jars. The delicate hook went up the nostril to start removing the brain.

Normally it would then be allowed to dry out with natron but this was the underworld and that didn't seem to be an issue as Anubis began to wrap the body. He wrapped each limb individually in strips of the finest linen before then wrapping them so they were secured into position, Ra's arms crossed across his chest in honour of the fact he had been a king of Egypt.

Out of the body rose Ra's ba, a bird with a human

head. It fluttered around the room like a real trapped bird. It paused as it spotted Cleo. Cleo instinctively held out a hand as if she was trying to entice a bird to eat from her palm. The ba looked too big to sit on her hand but when it did land there was barely any weight to it. It cocked it's head just like a bird would then chuckled, "what do you think?" Cleo's mouth fell open in shock.

Anubis looked over, his head on one side like a dog listening to its owner. He growled and the ba took off. It circled the room again, whooping, before sweeping past Cleo. Cleo turned, "where is it going? Shouldn't it stay with the body?"

"Not him my child." Sokar replied, "he is free for the moment and can do as he pleases."
Anubis growled again and picked up Ra's linen wrapped body and walked through a false door that appeared.

Cleo and Sokar followed Anubis down another corridor which was a stone cut passage and then out on to another cliff ledge. Ahead of them was a funerary sledge with the minor gods again at the ropes. There was a canopy over the bed held up by wooden poles carved into winged goddesses emulating the winged goddesses on a sarcophagus. Anubis gently placed the mummy of Ra on the bed.

On the other side of the funerary sledge the cliff dropped away. Looking down she saw a dry riverbed and beyond that another cliff. A paved road weaved down the cliff they were on, across the riverbed and then zig-zagged up the other side. What could be just about heard was the sound of thundering water, lots of water, and she wondered if the riverbed below was about to flood. She turned as Sokar called to her. The sledge was ready to go.

HOUR 5

Cleo stared in horror at the white topped mass of water descending into a black pit. It was like a waterfall on a river in spate. On the other side of the cascading water was another palace or temple entrance identified by the two large pylons. Carved across the stonework were lions chasing an unidentified enemy.

The spray soaked Cleo, causing the dress to cling to her body. It made her hair frizzy and created a thin film on her exposed skin. It was a shower she hadn't wanted. Looking to the gods none of them were affected by the spray. They stood tall and untouched making Cleo huff in frustration and pull the clinging fabric away from her body.

Crossing the chasm was a pair of scales. The beams of the scales were made of the arms of Ma'at, the goddess of Truth, Justice and Balance. Her body was part of the pillar as she balanced on a tall tower of stone that the waters were crashing around. Hanging from her horizontal arms were large metal shallow dishes.

The gods pulling the mortuary sledge hesitated. They had never seen Ma'at so chaotic. Normally it was as still as a reflecting pool in a temple with not a ripple on the surface. Thoth shouted over the sound of the thundering water, "keep going!"
The gods reluctantly began pulling the sledge on to the first pan, glancing down at the raging water.

They were all on the first half of the scales when a wind swept up from the tumbling mass of water and lifted the scale's pan, making the ropes holding it slack. The gods pulling the sledge hunkered down with moans of fear. Ra's mummified body began to slip. Sokar let out a yelp and pushed it back on to the wooden sledge. The others fell to their knees and hoped the pan wouldn't tip any further as the wind fell away and the pan dropped and erratically swung.

Cleo spread her feet to brace herself against the swinging. Although she could feel the dish swaying it was like she was in a different place. She wasn't feeling the same effects that the immortals were.

They were clinging tight to the base of the pan or to the sledge. Sokar was lying over Ra's body. He called out, "what is Ma'at up to?!"

"This has to be Apep." Isis cried out while clinging to her sister, "how can we stop this?"

Thoth looked over at Cleo who was standing unaffected, "he's ignoring her. Cleopatra, we need your help."

Cleo's eyes widened. She pointed at herself, "me?"

"Apep doesn't care about you. We need you to climb up and stop Ma'at's arms from swinging."

Cleo looked up and saw Ma'at's face grimacing as she struggled to control the swinging pans. The goddess leant back as the wind blew up the length of her body and into her face. Her beam arms see-sawed because of all the weight being only on one pan.

Cleo looked down at the waters that swirled round the rock pillar like water going down a plughole. She looked at Thoth, "how do I stop her?"

"You need a pin just like a normal set of scales. You should know that."

Cleo bit her lip to stop herself retorting back she didn't need to know that. That's what digital scales were for. Instead she said, "I haven't got anything to use as a pin."

"Get up there and I will throw a spear up to you."

"What spear?"

"I will create one." Isis snapped, "now get up there."
Cleo took a step back. She looked at the ropes and couldn't
see herself climbing it. It wasn't something she could do
when the gym equipment was unfolded from the wall,
"don't you sometimes have wings? You could fly up."

"Not in this wind. Get on with it you useless khat."
Nephthys snapped in her sister's defence, "you need to
make yourself useful so start climbing." She fiercely
pointed at the rope.

Cleo huffed before crossing to one of the ropes.
What had from a distance looked like a smooth rope of flax
turned out to have knots in it which would make it easier to
climb if it wasn't for her attire. She didn't think the real
Cleopatra would ever have been found climbing in the
sheath dress she was currently wearing. She didn't even
want to think about the fact she wasn't wearing any
knickers! Would the gods even be bothered? She glanced at
them and decided they were nothing like the amorous
Greek and Roman gods. She sidled up to Thoth and quietly
asked, "do you have a knife?"
He frowned at her, "a knife?"

"I can't climb in this." She gestured at her dress.
Thoth nodded in understanding. He pulled a knife out from
nowhere and handed it to her. She used the flint blade to
cut a long slit in the linen dress before removing her
sandals.

Carefully she pulled herself up on to the rope and
felt for a knot with her bare foot. She paused halfway up, a
foot slipping on a knot as the wind whirled around her. She
clung to the rope trying not to whimper. This was the
craziest thing she had ever done and it had to be in her
head. Never would she want to go on a zipwire or do a
treetop rope course again.

The wind whipped her skirt up but she couldn't
release her hold to push it down. She hoped none of the

gods were looking up as she had her Marilyn Monroe moment.

The wind wasn't dying down so with gritted teeth she began to pull herself up the rest of the rope, one knot at a time. Suddenly there was a hand in front of her. She hesitated a moment before grabbing hold of it. She found herself hauled up and straddling the beam.

Behind her were the cliffs of Sokar's necropolis home and his step pyramid. Ahead of her, past Ma'at's ostrich feathered headdress, beyond the pylons, was the palace or temple they had to get to. Foolishly she looked down and saw the swirling torrents of water, eroding the rock pillar Ma'at's feet precariously balanced on. She looked away and caught Ma'at's expression. Ma'at was grimacing and straining to keep her scales balanced. Cleo asked, "do I really have to pierce you with a spear?"

"Do it. I can't keep it steady forever." The goddess said through gritted teeth.

The wind had followed Cleo up as if it had realised what was happening. It swept through Ma'at's feather headdress and tugged at Cleo's hair, blinding her.

"Okay." Cleo said slowly to herself to calm her nerves. She took a breath in before shouting down, "give me the spear."

"Thoth, tell her to get on with it." Nephthys snapped.

"Ladies, calm yourselves." Thoth retorted, "this is Apep's doing remember."

"Nephthys take a deep breath." Isis said, "we need to have faith and not let Apep get to us."

"She's my wife remember." Thoth remarked, "you are asking that khat to harm her."

"We need to get Ra safely across. I'm sorry Thoth, but as you know, he is more important than your wife." Sokar said as he still lay over Ra's wrapped body.

"Fine." Thoth huffed. He put his hands together and

pulled them apart, producing a spear between them. He threw it up to Cleo who miraculously, for her, caught it.

Cleo adjusted her hold on the spear and then carefully stood on the beam. Facing Ma'at she asked, "where do I put this?"

"Just below my throat, hurry."

She tried to recall if she had ever held a javelin and had a feeling that even at her Comprehensive the boys wouldn't have been trusted and it had been a good one. She hefted the heavy spear up and held it in both hands, flint tip pointed at Ma'at's sternum. She hoped she had the strength to break through the bone.

As she thrust it through the bone at Ma'at's throat the goddess' mouth opened in a silent scream. Below, Thoth let a tear drop from his eye. Isis reached out a hand to him and murmured, "I will look after her."

With lips pressed together he nodded stiffly. He had to remember this was because of Apep. He knew a form of Isis would heal his wife once they were clear of the scales.

As the beams abruptly stopped Cleo was thrown into Ma'at's face. Thoth shouted up, "well done. You can come down now."

With the wind gone the air was still and peaceful where Cleo was and she took a moment to sit and take it all in. Had she really just speared a goddess who looked like a set of scales?

Below Thoth stood with hands on hips looking up at her while Isis and Nephthys cautiously stood up and hurried across the invisible bridge linking the two pans and the far side. The gods pulling Ra's sledge slowly got up and began pulling as Sokar jumped on the back and held Ra in place, just in case. Thoth was the last to leave as he watched Cleo slowly descend the rope, ready to catch her if needed, but he was also worrying about the next few minutes. With Sekhmet out with Hathor stalking Apep who

would whisper the secret spell to allow them to pass
through to Amentet's palace?

Cleo was relieved to reach what was terra firma.
Thoth put a hand on her shoulder, "thank you."

"That was the scariest thing I have ever done." She
replied as she tried to shake out her trembling limbs. The
adrenalin was dissipating.

"Come on, we have lingered here long enough and we
have a meeting we can't miss." He strode away leaving
Cleo staring. Was he angry at her for what she had had to
do? He had been so friendly towards her before this
moment. Or was it the stress of the situation?

They might have been in a hurry but Cleo couldn't
help staring up at the two carved pylons that made her think
of the Ramesseum. One had a giant lioness running after
rows of an enemy. On the other sat a lioness headed
Sekhmet seated side on receiving offerings from her fellow
immortals. However, that was the only things surviving
from Apep. She could see where Apep had dragged his way
through like the rope marks on a bridge by the canal.

They crossed an open to the air central court. It was
pitch black above their heads. Their way was lit by flaming
torches on stakes in the paved floor close to high pillars
that reminded Cleo of pictures of Karnak. Some had been
blown out creating pockets of darkness.

From the central court they stepped through double
doors that had been flung open, one even hung off its hinge
at an awkward angle. Stepping into the columned hall she
gagged at the stench. Amongst chunks of masonry from the
ceiling and painted walls were dismembered bodies of lions
strewn across the floor. The horrific smell came from the
blood sprayed across the walls and puddled on the floor,
and the sulphuric scented lion dung. She stepped back out,

her mouth open to gulp down mouthfuls of fresh air.

She took a deep breath and stepped back inside so she wasn't left behind. She stepped to Sokar's side. He glanced at her and pointed down a dark passageway on the other side of the room, "that's where we need to go."
A magic seal had been thrown carelessly to the floor and the door it had protected had been smashed open.
Behind a hand covering her nose with some of her skirt, Isis remarked, "at least Sekhmet is out with Hathor. It could have been a lot worse."

"She won't like this." Sokar commented.

"Can we keep moving please." Nephthys said while glancing round nervously at both the bodies and the groove in the floor.

The smell followed them through into the dark passage not helped by the sledge having been dragged through the dung and bodies. At the other end of the passage they stepped into a new room that felt more intimate. The dark blue ceiling of gold stars was held up by two pillars painted to look like lotus flowers. On the floor before them Amentet's jackal headed guard lay dead, red welts round his body where Apep had squeezed the life out of him.

The sledge came to a stop halfway out of the passage so that everyone had to squeeze pass. Nephthys spoke first, "how is this place untouched?"

"Not completely." Sokar cocked his head at the body on the ground, "and where is Amentet?"
There was a whimper from behind the empty throne on its dais. The immortals all looked to Cleo. She wasn't going to be missed if she died. Nephthys said, "khat, go and find out who is behind the chair."
Cleo rolled her eyes. Where were the strong indominable gods of Egypt?

She crossed the room, pausing to look out of a pillar

framed balcony. Amentet's palace was situated just beyond the black silts of the underworld's version of the Nile. She could see something was amiss, kas stood holding tools gathered in groups looking at the extremely narrow strip of black silt either side of the river.

She was brought back to the room when she heard a nervous voice from behind the wooden chair, "hello?" Cleo turned to see a young woman emerging from behind the gold painted wooden armed chair which was on a dais. The cushion on it was half falling off as if someone had left the chair in a hurry. Her linen dress was torn but otherwise she appeared unharmed. Her headdress was in one hand.

Isis and Nephthys ran to her and embraced her. Amentet looked around, "what is going on? Was that Apep?"
Everyone looked up as they heard the cry of a kite and down from the beams one flew down to land on Amentet's wrist. In its beak was her Ankh, a cross with a loop in the top of it, the symbol of life. She stroked the raptor with the back of a finger as she whispered, "thank you."
She took the ankh back as Thoth replied, "he's escaped. Hathor and Sekhmet are stalking him."

"Are you alright Amentet?" Isis asked, running her hands over Amentet's body, "were you hurt?"

"I managed to hide as he came through the passage. Wepwawet tried to fight him off but it was futile. Amenset took my ankh and hid away so he couldn't find them." She smiled at the kite. She looked up again, "he didn't linger."

"That's good." Thoth remarked.

"Hopefully the newly dead managed to hide. Hurry up and get him back under control otherwise no one is safe. And Ra?" She glanced over at the sledge.
Cleo found herself wanting to point out that all the newly dead were currently waiting in line to have their hearts weighed and they were definitely safe.

"He is fine but we must hurry on down to the depths now we know you are safe. Will you open the doors for us?"

"Of course." She crossed the room, pausing to put a hand on her guard who stirred and the red welts faded.

She held out a hand and he gratefully took it as he reached for his spear with its broken shaft and then was pulled up. He followed her to a pair of double doors that had an intact seal. She put a hand on it and murmured a spell. The seal glowed and then was absorbed into the doors as they opened.

HOUR 6:

The walls of the passage dissolved into a swirling fog on either side of a paved path with grooves worn into it from the sledge. Cleo, at the back, screamed as a hand stretched out from the cloudy mass and was pulled back in.

She had jumped as well and fell backwards landing on her bum. The entity, she decided that was what it was, pulsed and she could see ripples in it like a stone thrown into a pond.

"Get off the floor khat! You are making a nuisance of yourself!" Nephthys turned and glared at her.
Cleo pointed at the 'wall', "but…. But, didn't you see the hand." She looked down the corridor and saw others.

"The desperate." Nephthys scoffed.

Five minutes later Thoth and Sokar, leading the group stopped. Ahead could be heard fighting. They looked at each other and then back up the line. Cleo felt their eyes on her and felt the urge to hide. She was starting to think that she was going to be the easy option for the immortals. Send in the mortal, no one would miss her. And on cue Thoth called out down the line, "Cleo, come down here." Cleo sighed, straightened her back and then promptly lost all her courage as several hands appeared. She shuffled sideways down the side of Ra's funerary sledge, her back pressed against it.

Cleo fought the urge to bow her head like a servant

as she reached the gods, "yes?"

"We need you to go ahead again."

"Why? Am I that dispensable?" She retorted, recalling Nephthys' stinging words.

"You are not dispensable, but you are unseen." Sokar calmly replied, "you aren't meant to be here so no one sees you. All attention is on us as we protect Ra. You can slip in, see what is happening and then report back."

Cleo wanted to say no and stay with the immortals. Whatever was happening further on didn't sound good. She could hear the echoes of shouts coming up the passage. She asked, "do I get something to defend myself with?" Thoth reluctantly handed over his knife, "I want it back." Feeling like a petulant teenager she retorted, "whatever." She didn't have to care about them since within an hour this was the second time they were sending her into a dangerous situation.

She headed down the short passage and entered into a chamber lined with paintings of Ra's journey through the underworld, of his death and rebirth…. Except they weren't. The images were busy silently cheering and cringing with the fighting they were witnessing. Cleo turned from the wall paintings to see what they were all looking at.

In the chamber there was a group of pharaohs dressed for combat battling with a group of gold and black scaled Apeps. They wore bands of leather wrapped around their chests and wrists and held large cow hide covered shields.

One was wrapped in the coils of one of the snakes as two of the pharaohs akhs stabbed at it with spears. Finally it gave up its victim of choice reluctantly and slithered off to nurse its wounds.

One of the snakes spotted her and rose up like a cobra, hissing at Cleo, pressing her against the wall. She closed her eyes against the revealed fangs. She stuck out the knife and hoped, luck, anything, would save her from death by mythological snake.

The hissing stopped as she felt a weight on the knife, pulling her hand down. She opened her eyes to see the body of the snake slipping off the knife. The blade and her hand were now sticky with blood. Out of the corner of her eye she saw the painted gods clapping at her while another was pointing and laughing. She stepped away from the wall to see what the painted figure was laughing at and saw she had been pressed against one of the images who was now squashed, arms and legs spread like a Hanna-Barbera cartoon character. She tried not to giggle herself even though she was in a dangerous situation.

Remembering where she was she went to report back hoping Thoth and Sokar would come and support the pharaoh akhs. She was stopped in her tracks by the sound of scales scratching on the floor. She should have just run but instead she slowly turned.

The mini Apeps had noticed her and were now gathered behind her, rising up so their heads were at the same height as her's, growing thicker and bigger to support themselves. So much for being invisible! She held out the knife in desperation but she found herself frozen to the spot, mesmerised by the slowly swaying heads. Was she being hypnotised? Would the royal akhs save her?

The pharaohs, their breaths caught, agreed to work as a team now that all the Apeps' attention was on someone else. At the pharaohs shouting a battle cry Cleo closed her eyes expecting death by either snake or pharaoh. She decided this was too ridiculous to even be a dream just as there was a feline roar, echoed by another. Leaping into the fray came two red pawed lionesses.

60

Cleo decided it was safer on the floor while large paws and two mouths full of sharp teeth grabbed the writhing snakes and flung them around. The akhs flattened themselves against walls, the paintings peering over shoulders and round bodies.

The snakes fought back, hissing and striking out at the two lionesses. They were no match for the two goddesses who tore the snakes from their limbs, not bothered at all by the fangs and wounds that dripped blood. They bit down on the snakes so the serpent bodies hung limp in their mouths before giving them a good shake and then throwing the body away in disgust.

The last mini Apep was dead and the lionesses roared their triumphant. The akhs fell to their knees and bowed their heads. The lionesses snarled at the akhs before stepping over Cleo and stalking up the passage. One paused to sniff at Cleo's body, snorted and continued on.

Ra's sledge appeared and once in the room the gods who had been pulling it stepped away, bowed to it and disappeared. The paintings became still in anticipation of what was coming. Cleo slowly stood just as the torches round the room flickered and then went out with a serpentine hiss. Nephthys squeaked and Isis grabbed her arm and hissed, "ssh."

Everyone, including Cleo and the pharoah akhs, moved closer to the sledge as they heard scales rubbing on stonework and sensed a large presence. Apep was making his presence known.

With a flash of light that caused everyone to squint a small flame appeared cupped in the hands of Sekhmet. She appeared as a woman dressed in a red linen sheaf dress with the mask of a lioness pushed on to her forehead. The flame grew as she softly blew on it and then with a big puff of breath it split up and flew to the extinguished torches. With an angry hiss Apep's presence disappeared, slithering off into the darkness where he was safe. The bodies of his miniatures also disappeared.

Sekhmet remarked grimly, "now it is safe."

"Let us prepare for our lord's rebirth then." Sokar said, standing straight and shaking off the fact he had been as scared as the others. This wasn't the first time, nor would it be the last, that Apep made his presence known but it didn't mean it would ever get any easier. He looked round, "where is Aker? Without him Ra's ka can not return and regenerate."

"I saw his tracks while we were out stalking." Hathor commented as she appeared beside her twin sister. She looked at Cleo with an arrogance to her expression, her nose slightly up, a raised eyebrow.

"Let's hope he can keep the Eastern border protected as otherwise Ra can't be reborn." Sokar said with a frown.

There was a growl and a deep voice remarked, "of course it is. How dare you insignificant youths even think it. I am older than Ra so give me the respect I am due."

"Aker?" Isis called out. She bowed, "please forgive us ancient one. We didn't mean to offend you."

"Apep is chaos. He does not need much to free himself to cause trouble. Now, I see two of you are injured." Out of the flickering shadows stepped a lion and Cleo instantly thought of Aslan. It took her a minute to realise that the brown and yellow mane framed face was human not feline. He looked at her, but it felt like he was looking through her. He turned away from her and continued, "my twin watches the east side and it is quiet for now. Apep is following you or staying one step ahead it seems."

"We know." Hathor retorted, her hands fists and her beautiful face briefly becoming an angry lioness.

"Excuse me." Thoth interrupted, "but have any of you

seen Ra's ba?"

"No, but it won't be long." Aker replied knowingly.

With a whoop of, "look out below!" Ra's human headed, bird bodied ba flew down. He landed on the mummified body as Sokar approached and initiated the opening of the mouth ceremony with his ceremonial blade made of bone. With Ra's mouth figuratively re-opened the ba shrank and was reabsorbed.

The body within the linen wraps began to shrink and then to move. There was a giggle like there was a child hiding under the blanket of a bed waiting to be found. There was childish grunt as the bandages wiggled and then a child's shaven head, apart from a plaited sidelock, appeared and shouted, "BOO!"
Sokar pretended to be surprised as the child Ra giggled with pleasure. Gently Sokar said, "come my lord, there are akhs here to see you."

"Do I have to?" Ra sighed as he turned his thin legs round to hang off the edge of the mortuary sledge where he swung them.

"Yes." Aker answered sternly, "they have fought to protect you this night. Acknowledge them."
Ra looked at the ancient god and tried to look resentful of being told what to do. He pouted and crossed his arms, "fine."
The pharaohs approached and bowed before the boy who looked more bemused than anything else.

Like any other child he quickly got bored. His eyes glazed over at the pharaohs murmuring words of praise and he began to look at everyone present. He stared at Cleo as she was someone he had never seen before. He pointed at Cleo, "who is she?"

Sokar beckoned Cleo forward who was also staring

back at the child god. Sokar said, "sir, this is Cleopatra."

"You look different." Ra frowned.

"There were many Cleopatras and many more named in honour of them." Cleo said.

"Do you like to play?" Ra asked, his mind already moved on.

"Play?"

"Yes." Ra slipped off the sledge and took Cleo's hand, "you look like someone who likes to play."

Cleo looked at Sokar.

The god shrugged his shoulders, "this is where my duties end. I have seen him safely through his death to his rebirth. Take care of him." He chuckled as Cleo was dragged along by Ra towards a wall that opened up to reveal a passage as they approached.

Sokar and Aker watched as the passage sealed itself up behind Thoth. There was no evidence of it once it was closed, not even a seam in the painting. Aker sighed and sank to the ground, his front paws stretched out in front of him. Sokar frowned, "what is wrong old friend?"

Aker looked up, exhaustion now etched across his face, "have I failed him?"

"What do you mean?"

"My other half, in the east, he fought hard but is wounded. That is how Apep got out but I wasn't going to tell them that."

"You did the right thing not telling them. Now go bring you brother to me so he can be reborn."

Aker nodded and then disappeared.

Sokar turned and headed back up the passage, out of the tomb.

HOUR 7

Osiris sat on this throne with Mehen curled round the dais, tongue flickering in and out as his beady eyes stared at the men knelt before Osiris. Sitting to one side was a baboon with a scribe's palette at his knee. The three men were bound in rope with their hands tied behind their backs. They wore torn jeans and trainers and t-shirts. Their skin was smeared with dust. Though she couldn't see their faces Cleo knew they were from her time and were probably feeling as bewildered as she was. Somehow they had died raiding a tomb or buried temple and now were before Osiris.

Standing over them with short staffs held in their hands, were two demons, part man, part animal, like their sister Ammet who resided in the Hall of Truth. They had the long beaks of an ibis, the body of men, but the back legs of a hippo, hideous things made to scare people.

Ra, who in the space of time it had taken to walk the length of the secret passage, had become a straight-backed youth on the cusp of adulthood, paused at the edge of the room to watch the scene along with his immortals companions and Cleo. He knew his destiny and his responsibilities but he was also aware that the night was different. He had noted the blood on Hathor that needed to be cleaned off and he noted the khat who accompanied them wide eyed in bewilderment and awe at everything.

The court was in session and Osiris acknowledged their presence with the barest of nods. He knew they were all simply passing through to reach the riverbank. He didn't react as Thoth slipped down the side of the room and peered over the baboon scribe's shoulder to see what he was recording. The baboon looked up and they gave each other a nod before Thoth left him.

Once back at the group Cleo looked questioningly at Thoth. Thoth whispered, "They died violating a burial place. Their hearts don't deserve to be weighed. They would fail. They will be judged here and a decision made by Osiris. This is Apep. He can infect anyone."

"Infect? They were probably just after money to feed their families."

"You are kind hearted. They had money and wanted more." He said sternly and then softened his tone, "have you ever had a moment when you have felt so angry or crazy and everyone around you is confused why?"

"I suppose."

"You were that one bit closer to chaos at that point." Thoth replied with a solemn tone, "even Hathor and Sekhmet have been touched by him many times."

Cleo remembered then the tales that were told of a blood thirsty Hathor or Sekhmet, depending upon the version, killing a village of people on Ra's orders. But they didn't stop once they had tasted the blood of man. To stop them Thoth had been sent for and he had dyed a puddle of beer red to make them so drunk they forgot their blood thirst. She realised then that everyone who had had too much on a Friday night in a uni town would have been touched by Apep's chaotic nature.

She realised then how important Ma'at was, even in the modern age, even if it didn't go by that name anymore. Without her keeping the world in balance chaos truly would rule and currently it was fighting for every centimetre of balance against Apep and his reign of chaos. She looked at Thoth and he was smiling at the fact she had just realised. He asked, "what do you call ma'at now?"

"I don't know, peace, prosperity." She shrugged, she didn't really know as her world was in turmoil at the moment.

"Without Ra and Ma'at there would never be peace. That is why every night we fight Apep to keep him weak."

"Even though no one worships you anymore?" Cleo interrupted.

"You know who we are though." He raised a knowing eyebrow, "now… Every thought, every action that causes an imbalance in the world fuels him and makes him stronger."

"So if they are only being influenced by Apep is it fair they are being punished? If just knowing and researching about all of you is keeping you alive why is there a queue of kas who haven't gone through the Hall of Two Truths for centuries? Shouldn't they be filtering through?" Her voice was rising.

"Ssh." Thoth hissed.

"Well?" She whispered.

"What do you think? They still killed or stole something they shouldn't have. They could have resisted his whispers."

"What will happen to them?"

"They were tomb robbers."

"How did they get past the weighing of the heart?"

"They haven't got there. They came straight here."

"Were they pulled out of the line by those hands?"

"More than likely. They didn't heed their elders' warnings and found themselves stumbling into a trap in a tomb. Greed got the better of them. Now, we continue on. The boat will be waiting for us on the other side and we will be travelling by water again." He gestured across the chamber to a dark gap between two pillars.

It was as if there was an invisible screen between the scene and the travellers. No one looked up, no one turned, as they crossed at the back of the chamber. Both Ra and Cleo turned as there was the thwack of a wooden staff on a bare back. Ra winced. Thoth murmured to the youth, "it has to be done."

"I feel sorry for them. Apep tempted them." Ra remarked with a sorrowful tone.

"Apep didn't tempt them. Human emotions are involved as well, greed, survival, the need to save a loved one. We don't know why they broke into a tomb." Cleo exclaimed and resisted added, 'we don't know how they even found it.'

"Enough." Thoth turned on Cleo, "there is a rhythm to the night which must be followed. You are not here to judge us or question our ways. You are here on sufferance."

"We'll be glad to see the back of you." Nephthys added.

☥

They walked away leaving Cleo glaring at them with clenched fists. She didn't want to be here anymore than they wanted her. She wanted to wake up from this nightmare either in a hospital bed or at least lying in the fallen plasterwork of the sweltering tomb. She fought the urge to stamp her foot and shout a retort. The sound of scales on a hard surface sent her running after the immortals.

☥

They all blinked in the light being admitted by Ra as if he had just remembered he was the Sun God. The light revealed they were on the river bank of the underworld's Nile. The light also drew out the kas who had passed the test within the Hall of Two Truths. They all carried a feather of Ma'at as proof, some holding them tight in fear of losing it and being eaten by the crocodile jawed Ammet. Others were holding their feathers as if it was the most

68

fragile thing they had ever held.

Cleo came running out of the passage, was instantly blinded, and crashed into a group of kas who with shouts of horror fell into the Nile as Thoth reached for Cleo and grabbed her flaying arm. He pulled her to his chest where she gasped at all the muscles she felt and the fact she had been so close to falling in the river. Then she remembered she was angry with him and pushed him away, "get off me."

She looked round then, feeling eyes on her and saw the kas staring at her while others were rescuing the ones from the Nile. She stuttered, "how…. How… how are there still kas travelling when no one has moved on the other side?"

She turned on the spot as she watched the kas split around them like the group were a rock diverting a river's flow. She realised then that they were hazy round the edges. They were ghosts or memories. She turned to see where the kas were going. They were heading along the bank, using the light of Ra to see by.

She turned away when she heard angry voices. She couldn't understand what was being said but she could see a new group of minor gods at the prow of the barge and one of them was gesturing at Ra and then at the water he stood in. Cleo sidled up to Nephthys reluctantly and asked, "what are they saying?"

"They say the water is lower than normal." The goddess replied before realising who had asked and stepped away with a scowl.

Cleo turned to Thoth, "Thoth, the boat looks like it's still floating."

"That is what he's telling him." Nephthys snapped, arms crossed, then turned back away with a sniff.

Thoth turned to look at everyone, "everyone get on board. We are leaving now. We can't keep delaying."

Cleo glanced down at the Nile as she crossed the plank

from the riverbank on to the barge, another boat made of bundles of reeds. She had a feeling the water level had dropped. She could see the dark line where the water normally reached along with algae but the water was below the line. Was the boat riding high or had the water level dropped like the gods had said?

Before long the boat began to scrap along the riverbed. Then it ground to a halt. Ahead of them was a sinkhole lined with rocks that looked suspiciously like fangs. The last of the water poured into it leaving the boat sitting in a long deep puddle of silt.

The immortals ran to the front. Never had the water levels fallen so low that the boat became grounded. Not even hiding Ra and his glowing body to fool Apep would work here. They needed Apep to regurgitate the water, but how?

The riverbed began to undulate as if it was no longer rock and silt.

Ra stepped out of his cabin where Thoth had told him to stay. The riverbed had become the body of a snake with black and white scales. In reaction to Ra's appearance Hathor span round and hissed, "get back in. It's not safe out here."

"What's going on?" The youthful Ra asked.

"Apep is trying to stop us from carrying on." Thoth answered, "you need to get back inside before he comes for you."

"Hathor you are meant to protect him. What are you going to do?" Nephthys turned to the Eye of Ra with an accusing look.

Hathor looked at Ra and then at Cleo, cocking her head and being watchful of the khat, seeing if there was any sign of Cleo being influenced by Apep. Cleo couldn't look the goddess in the eye and looked away. Hathor smirked as she turned away. She crossed to the side of the boat and looked down at the quivering muscles of the serpent as it tensed at scenting Ra.

The adrenalin was rising in Hathor and she glanced over to her sister Sekhmet and saw twitching face muscles and knew she was keen as well. They nodded at each other in mutual understanding. They didn't need to talk to plan and work together. They turned to look at Cleo.

Apep was too strong for Hathor and Sekhmet to take him on without weakening him first. To attack him they needed a distraction, and Cleo was a dispensable khat, an ideal distraction. Hathor looked to Isis and said, "give her extra strength."

"What are you planning?" Isis frowned, "you need to tell us so we can prepare."

"Just do as I say if you want Ra to survive." Hathor retorted and then broke off a loose reed from the boat. She concentrated on it and it grew thicker, longer and heavier till it was a spear.

Cleo was distracted by Hathor creating the spear and jumped when Isis took her hands and held them tight in hers. She tried to pull away, "hey! What are you doing?"

"Ssh. Hathor will explain in a minute." Isis, adjusting her hold on her hands.

She couldn't help staring and becoming still as she saw Isis begin to glow, gradually descending through her body to her hands. Her hands began to grow warm and that warmth headed up her arms. She felt her muscles go tense and then grow. She looked at her arms and saw her skin stretching over the individual muscles, bulking out her biceps and shoulder muscles.

Isis smiled as she stepped away and declared, "she's ready."

"Good. Cleo?" Hathor said.

"Yes." She answered warily.

"With this spear," she held the spear out to Cleo, "you are going to pin Apep down by his neck."

"I'm not Steve Backshall!" Cleo protested.

"Who?" Hathor frowned.

"Never mind. Why can't you do this?"

"Because once Apep is pinned down Sekhmet and I can come in. We cannot continue on until Apep regurgitates the water. Understand?" She retorted.

Cleo took a step away from Hathor as she reluctantly took the spear from the goddess. She was surprised at the weight of it. No wonder Isis had had to make her stronger. The next thought that came to her was she wanted to say no and run away from the craziness but there was nowhere to go.

She was stuck on a boat, which was stuck on top of a snake. She was trapped in this insane experience. Reluctantly she nodded, "yes."

"Good, let's go." Hathor and Sekhmet led the way to the front of the boat and climbed up on to the edge of it, either side of the carved lotus plant prow.

Below them the gods holding the ropes were clinging to them as they tried to find purchase on Apep's scales. Hathor pointed forward, "over there, towards the mouth. Pin him there. Either that will be enough to get him to spit up all the water or our attack will be ready."

Cleo wanted to say no again. She looked out at the serpent and then back at Ra then took a deep breath in. Was this her moment to play at being a hero? Her Tomb Raider moment? And no one would ever know. She gave a nod as she knew if she said anything it would be a negative.

"Get on with it then."

She pulled herself up on to the edge of the boat next to Sekhmet. She had a feeling Hathor would just push her off if she was next to her. Sekhmet murmured, "you can do this."

Cleo glanced at her and she had a feline smile. She could imagine her as a farm cat hunting mice and rats amongst the strawbales with a torn ear.

She looked out at Apep's long back and tried to decide if this was more insane then climbing Ma'at and stabbing her. She would decide later when this was all over, if it did end. With a deep breath she jumped down on to Apep's broad back. She didn't linger as she scrabbled to her feet and began running down Apep's bucking back.

She had never run so well in her life so had assumed Isis' blessing had affected more than just her arm muscles. She leapt over one of the pulling gods as it got in the way like she was in a hurdles race.

She leapt again, higher than was feasibly possible, lifting her spear high, point down. She felt like Bodicca! Apep bucked upwards, water sloshing in his wide open mouth. With a shout of "cowabunga!" She thrust the spear into Apep's neck, putting all her weight behind it. She pressed down hard, pushing the speak deeper into Apep's flesh. It seemed to grow longer so it ended up in the riverbed, pinning him like a butterfly collector would pin their new butterfly.

Apep couldn't voice his anger as he was bloated with water but that didn't stop him from thrashing. He flicked his length in tight twists in an attempt at loosening the huge bronze headed spear. Cleo clung tight to the spear. She didn't dare look round to see what the goddesses were doing.

Behind her Hathor and Sekhmet leapt from the boat, large knives in their hands. They roared their arrival and slowed their descent to the riverbed with sharp claws scratching through Apep's scales. Apep's body turned to retreat away from the claws but the water inside him was acting like an anchor.

With their own battle cry the two sister goddesses stabbed their knives into Apep's flesh. Water began to flow out of the wounds. They looked at each other and each knew what the other was thinking.

Sekhmet became a lioness and with the large flint knife in her mouth jumped over Apep's body. On the other side she changed back to her goddess form. In prefect sync with each other they stabbed their knives into Apep. But instead of pulling them out they began to run towards the boat, dragging their knives through Apep's side. Water began to pour out of Apep.

Apep's body contracted and then he heaved. The motion threw Cleo off the spear and she fell with a splash into the rising water. She staggered to her feet coughing and spluttering as the water rose around her.

The water coming out of Apep became a torrent which caught Hathor and Sekhmet in it and they were washed away. Cleo's legs were swept from under her and with a scream she disappeared into the foaming water as well, struggling to find her way back to the surface.

The boat rose on a wave of water and was carried forward on the crest of it, the minor gods now pressed against the prow looking terrified.

HOUR 8

Spinning and tossed around the barque crashed into boulders while travelling along what was normally rapids and had now turned into a serious of cascading drops before falling over the edge of a waterfall. The passengers onboard clung to everything they could and coughed up water as the barque bobbed back to the surface. They slowly stood up, wringing water from their clothes as the minor gods pulled the barque to shore.

Further down Hathor, Sekhmet and Cleo pulled themselves on to shore. The goddesses were miserable looking half drowned cats. They shook themselves, spraying water everywhere. Cleo lay on her back with her legs and arms sprawled around her. Hathor looked down at Cleo and began to giggle and then to laugh. Both Cleo and Sekhmet looked at each other and then at Hathor before beginning to laugh as well, so much so that Cleo had to clutch her stomach.

Ra strolled over to them once he had disembarked and looked curiously at the three of them, his head cocked like a bird. With a curious tone he asked, "what are you laughing about?"

"Noth… Nothing." Hathor's hysteria began to subside and she held out a hand to Cleo, "that was great work, thank you."

Cleo uncurled herself as a hiccup came out of her mouth. She blushed. How could she be hiccupping at a time like this, just as Hathor had acknowledged her? She accepted the held-out hand and was pulled to her feet. Sekhmet embraced her, "you did so well."

"Thank you." Cleo replied as she took in her surroundings.

They were in a huge cavern hollowed out by the waterfall which was so large she couldn't see all of it. Ra only lit up a small portion of it where he stood by the edge of the waterfall pool. The waterfall itself had become a trickle since carrying the barque over the edge. A few scales from Apep floated in the pool of water. Cleo asked, "where are we?"

"In the oldest part of the underworld. You have arrived at the point where Ra arose." A voice spoke, "come forward khat."

Cleo looked round for the owner of the voice and found herself staring at Thoth who had an amused smile on his face. She wasn't sure whether it was from her hiccups or from her reaction to the mystery voice.
He said, "go on, you won't be harmed." He pointed in a direction and Cleo saw a faint glow which was being reflected off the rock as if the ceiling of cavern was coming down to meet the ground.

Everyone else stayed by the shoreline as Cleo slowly, picking her way past large stalagmites, aimed towards the glow.

In the light of several flickering torches were sat five immortals on armed high-backed chairs with a table laden with food in front of them. Two sat as close as the chairs would let them, holding hands and didn't even bother looking at Cleo. They were Geb and Nut.

Nut was in a linen shift dress dyed dark blue with stars twinkling on it. Geb's goose was snuffling on the floor, pecking at the grain that had been scattered there. They were staring into each other's eyes and occasionally kissing each other. Geb kept trying to put his hand on Nut but the chair arms were stopping him.

As Cleo took it all in Nut got up and sat in Geb's lap, being pulled round the chair arms by him. His arms went around her and held her tight as his hands swept up the goddess' back and into her hair. Their kisses became more passionate and she wondered if they would ever stop.

Sat in the centre was Amun, slouched in his chair, almost as if he wanted to hook one leg over its arm. He had cobalt blue skin that glistened and on his head was a headdress with two feathers. He was chewing on a chunk of bread. He paused in his chewing, making Cleo think of a cow chewing its cud and he even had the long eyelashes. A word came to her, 'pretty boy'. With the attitude of a god who knew his importance he said, "do you know where you are khat? You should be honoured. I can't recall many living souls making this journey, if any."

"Leave her be." Shu remarked from where he was slumped in his chair, studying his nails. A feather in his hair identified him as the God of air, "our father chose to let her travel with him and be reborn. She's proven valuable so far, dispensable but valuable."

"Oh ssh." Tefnut, wearing her headdress of a solar disc encircled with the cobra Wadjet, said softly, "you are frightening her. She's risked her life twice and if she had died her ka would never see the Hall of Two Truths. It would go poof." She flicked the fingers of one hand apart to demonstrate.

Cleo wanted to find her voice and protest but she was struck dumb by who she stood before.

"Hmpfh." Shu responded and shifted in his chair.

"Well, she'd best return to the others before they think they can all parade through. Look at them over there, hovering and hoping I might let them approach." Amun remarked with a dismissive sniff.

"You were the one who called her over." Tefnut pointed

out, "you should at least give her a blessing."

"For what?"

Tefnut sighed and rolled her eyes.

"She is not troubled."

Cleo opened her mouth to object and suggest he looked to the kas waiting to be let through, maybe then he would act more like a benevolent god than a spoilt man.

"I wanted to see the oddity that was travelling with my son." Amun shrugged his shoulders, "where is Ra anyway?" He sat up in his chair properly and shouted, "Ra, get here now!"

The youthful Ra materialised beside Cleo and knelt before Amun, "oh Great Lord father Amun, thank you for creating me out of the primeval waters."

Amun waved a hand dismissively, "just get this khat back to where she belongs before Apep works out how to get down here. He doesn't yet and I want it to stay like that." He turned to Geb and Nut, "you two, enjoy this time wisely."

Geb and Net briefly paused in their kissing and Geb gave the barest of nods of acknowledgement. They knew that when Ra became the scarab in the sky then their father Shu would have to bear the weight of keeping them separate again. As for their children Osiris, Isis, Set and Nephthys, they were their own entities who the adult Ra had taken under his wing. Let him, they preferred each other's company more.

Ra stood and touched Cleo's arm, "come with me. Ignore them. They become bitter down here, shut away in the dark remembering that I, their true creator, leave them here."

Cleo frowned as she tried to remember her Egyptian mythology. At some point during the New Kingdom Amun and Ra had merged to be one god and two gods at the same time. Ra was the creator of the lands and the people and was considered the first pharaoh of Egypt. Amun had come from Kush with similar responsibilities so they were often considered Amun-Ra.

She wondered whether at the beginning there was more squabbling over who was top dog. The impression she had was a mutual ambivalence towards each other with a pretence of respect on some agreed routine. She looked over to Amun as she walked away from the five gods and he was sipping wine from a cup ignoring everyone as if he didn't care for anything but himself. She had the sense that as long as Ma'at was kept in balance he wouldn't get involved. He would leave Ra to do it all while he lazed with the others.

Cleo and Ra returned to the rest of the immortals still standing on the bank and Isis asked, "what did they want?"

"Nothing… I think." Cleo replied with a pensive look. Amun had wanted to see her and then had been dismissive of her.

"Don't worry about him. He can be a bit peculiar."

"That's what Ra said." Cleo looked at Ra who softly smiled.

Thoth interrupted, "we need to move on."

They followed the edge of the river, the waters of which were flowing upwards into a new cavern. Another path descended into the cavern and out of the gloom with a line of kas coming down it. The group's path and the kas' met where shabtis of blue faience, wood, plaster and ivory stood beside open chests. They moved stiff limbs to hand out clothes to the kas. Those who had been just buried in a simple hole in the sand were the most grateful for new clothes and stripped off there and then to put on the fresh linen kilts and dresses and stroked the fabric.

The kas continued on, entering another tunnel, where they began singing and it echoed in the enclosed space. It appeared none of them had a singing voice. To Cleo's ear it sounded more like yowling cats and wailing women. There was a background of humming which sounded primeval. Cleo thought of the idea of the mother goddess, Gaia, and that they were all returning to the womb before being 'reborn' in the Wernes. She knew that wasn't how the Egyptians thought but still that is what she was thinking.

They joined the line and followed them down the tunnel.

HOUR 9

Cleo was relieved when they cut down a narrow side tunnel. The bad singing and humming was starting to give her a headache and her wet dress was clinging to her in all the wrong places. And while she looked like a drowned rat the immortals looked like they hadn't been for a swim or been thrown off a waterfall in a boat. She tugged at the wet linen again with a grimace.

She looked up from her awkward walk because of the linen to see light at the end of the tunnel which now grew brighter with Ra's own glow. She heard music; music being created by instruments and not the awful caterwauling of the kas. She took a deep breath as she smelt food and her stomach grumbled.

They stepped into a colonnaded dining hall. In a U shape were set up tables and stools for everyone. To one side were the musicians playing a flute, harp and a drum. In the centre of the tables were several slender lithe Nubians wearing what looked like to Cleo beaded thongs. Their nipples were painted gold and they wore wide beaded collars. There were small bells at the ends of their plaited wigs. They were slowly twisting and turning in time to the music.

The tables were laid with food- roasted duck, whole steamed fish, pyramids of flat bread and fruit; bowls of wine soaked fruit and jugs of wine and beer. The smell was heady and Cleo could feel her mouth salivating.

Standing in front of it all was a falcon headed Horus with his arms stretched wide in welcome as he said loud enough to be heard over the music, "welcome to your hour of rest. Apep hasn't been here yet so for the moment you are safe. Sit, eat and enjoy the entertainment." He gestured to each side.

Ra took the spot at the head of the table with Hathor and Sekhmet on either side of him. There were no manners to be had from his daughters as they grabbed legs of duck and tore off chunks of bread and gulped down the watered wine. No one commented on their poor table manners. Thoth and Isis took one side of the table, once Horus had brushed aside his mother's need to embrace him.

Cleo hung back, unsure of whether she was allowed to join in the eating and drinking. She must have looked a little forlorn as Horus approached her, "come, sit and eat. You have earnt it as much as them."

"Even though I don't belong here?"

"Hathor has made you work hard and anyway this is a celebration. Ra has died and risen again and soon he will become the great scarab in the sky. Even us gods need some time to rest." He leant in and behind his hand he continued, "and talking to you delays me having to talk to my mother." He stepped back with a frown, "why are your clothes wet?"

"I went for a swim for Hathor."

"Here." Horus clicked his fingers and Cleo was now no longer standing in damp clothes.

She looked down to marvel at her new outfit which had the influence of the Greeks. She was now in a Greek chiton with a belt cinching in the fabric at her waist. Two safety pin like pins held the silk, this time, in place at her shoulders and to make the fabric the right length it had been pulled up under the belt and artfully draped on her chest. Her hair was piled up on her head and wrapped with a long strip of linen. Round her neck was a gold and pearl necklace and she had a bracelet with an enameled Eye of

Horus in it. She felt glamorous, like Elizabeth Taylor. She smiled at Horus.

Horus winked at her, "a queen has many outfits she can wear during the day."

"Thank you."

"Now, please, sit down and eat. If you have been working as hard as the sisters then you will be hungry." Horus beckoned Cleo to the table and poured her some beer and handed it to her.

"Thank you."

Hathor and Sekhmet were purring contentedly and looked as if they would fall asleep. Ra was leaning back in his chair lazily swirling the last of a glass of wine, one eye on the dancers while also looking like he was asleep. Isis and Nephthys were talking with Horus and Thoth was making notes on a piece of papyrus. Even Cleo was feeling lethargic after filling her belly with rich food.

It therefore took them all a moment to realise the music had abruptly stopped and they didn't even hear the musicians' squeaks of protest as they were killed by the knife welding akhs. The akhs' eyes were glazed over as if they didn't know what they were doing. With a growl they stepped over the bodies and headed towards the table.

The dancers screamed and fled as one of the attackers fell forward across the table between Horus and Isis with a spear in its back. Isis squeaked in alarm as a bronze sickle shaped sword appeared in her son's hand. Her eyes darted from the spear to the sword and back again. She recognised the ebony shaft of the spear to belong to her brother Set and feared he was trying to kill her son again.

With unearthly growls the other armed akhs charged at the tables scenting spilt blood. Horus leapt up, twisting round to face them, taking one out with his sword, just as Set appeared with another ebony shafted spear in his hand. Set sent it flying as more glazed eyed akhs came from the other side of the room. The atmosphere of the room began to feel like it was being squeezed.

Set shouted at his nephew, "protect Ra!"
Horus nodded, leapt on to the table and ran up it as with a roar Hathor and Sekhmet became lions and bounded over to the far side of the room.

Cleo did the only thing she thought was sensible and ducked under the table. She didn't want to be in this fight. She didn't want to be collateral damage of blood crazed gods and goddesses.

HOUR 10

The akhs were dead and everyone took a moment to catch their breaths and Cleo carefully emerged from under the table and crawled straight into a puddle of blood. She grimaced. Just her luck! She stood up just as Isis turned on her brother, "where have you been?!"
Set, with his long snouted, long eared Set animal head, scowled at his sister. Before he could answer, his nose twitched and the two lionesses growled.

Cleo looked round as the light had begun to change and the room was losing its definition. A mist rolled in, tumbling over like waves on the shore. She watched the immortals draw closer to Ra, who had turned from youth to young man, in the centre of them.

She edged closer to the group as, through brief gaps in the mist, she saw a scaly body moving. With a triumphant hiss the mist rose.

They all stood in the centre of a giant blue lotus flower. It floated on a swirling, bubbling mass of primeval water that they knew of as Nun. Slipping in and out of it were the scaled coils of Apep but no one could see his head as he slowly circled. Nephthys whispered, "What do we do?"

Isis looked round at everyone. Those that had already been fighting were already looking too tired and drained of energy to keep on. The khat just looked lost and she briefly felt sorry for Cleo who had ended up here in a bizarre twist of fate. Though Isis had the magic inside her to protect them all from knowing Ra's secret name she

wasn't sure whether it would help or hinder them. She took her sister's hand and murmured, "I can try."
Nephthys turned to Isis and squeezed both her sister's hands, "yes. We need a barrier to protect us or give the fighters some energy or…"
Isis looked to the others to see if they agree, "do I?"

"Go for it." Hathor replied as she licked the back of her hand and used it to wash blood from one of her feline ears.

Isis took a step away from the group who adjusted to keep Ra protected. She lifted her arms and began whispering a spell that as she repeated it her voice grew louder. A new light appeared above them, spreading out and descending.

Before it could touch the lotus flower Apep's tail whipped out of the water and hit Isis hard, causing her to fall. The barrier popped like a soapy bubble. Nephthys cried out and ran to her sister.

Horus shouted and in his anger at his mother being hurt his body grew and thickened as he turned into a huge red scaled cobra. The strong muscles of his coiled length held half of his length upright. His hood opened to reveal an imprint of a golden sun disc on his scales. A whisper of smoke drifted upwards from his open mouth which also held fangs dripping with venom.

Set smiled, his lips twisted in the smirk. He knew the boy had had it in himself to be more than just a mummy's boy, in both senses of the word. He watched, leaning on his spear, as Horus slipped into the primeval waters which began to boil around his body. The lotus flower bobbed back up to the surface from where it had sank because of the weight of Horus.

The waters swelled upwards as Apep swept towards Horus' red scaled serpent form. Soon the water was steaming and churning as the two snakes twisted round each other in an attempt to dominate the other.

The lotus flower began to buck and twist where it floated on the surface, held in place by its long stem. Everyone on the flower stumbled as they tried to keep their balance apart from Ra. He stood in the centre emitting the only light in the area. Thoth, from his knees, shouted, "we can't let Ra fall in."

Cleo looked up at Ra from where she lay on the lotus. She thought to herself he didn't look like he was going to be falling in any time soon. He looked positively serene standing there, legs shoulder width apart. The smile on his face suggested he was enjoying the thrill of being bounced up and down without any effort like a bouncy castle where everyone is bouncing and falling over apart from that one kid in the middle.

Hathor exclaimed, "what about the rest of us?!" She got on to her knees and was trying to stand up, "we are just as important! Let me at Apep." Her fists briefly became large lion paws.

"I am fine. Do what you need to do to stop Apep." Ra calmly replied as he watched the thrashing snakes as if it was normal to see a man become a snake and fight the demon snake of chaos.

Set stepped over, using his spear to stay upright, and pulled his wife and sister to their feet. He smirked, "I think this is where I step in to save everyone."

No one tried to disagree with him, not even Hathor and Sekhmet. Even they knew they couldn't do anything while Apep was in the water.

He finally noted Cleo's presence and thrust his spear at her, "hold this khat."

"What?!" Cleo managed to try and protest as she found herself holding Set's heavy spear. Thankfully Isis' added strength hadn't worn off. She watched wide eyed as he

slammed his hands together and then pulled them apart, producing a long papyrus rope. Without looking at Cleo he held out and hand and demanded, "spear."
Cleo gladly handed it back to him and watched as with a murmured spell the rope attached itself to the spear. Set looked at Cleo, "you any good at throwing?"

"N… no."
Set rolled his eyes, "what use are you then?"

"I'm not meant to be here."

"So you are Ra's pet tonight then?" He sneered.

"Does he often have people tag along like this?" Cleo asked out of curiosity. She ended with an "ouch!"
He had pinched her, hard, on her upper right arm as he commented, "that will have to do."

"What did you do to me?" Cleo exclaimed as she rubbed her arm.

"So there is a feisty person under there. I'm putting you to use. When I hold up my hand throw my spear to me."

"Umm… Sure."

"Excellent." He thrust the spear back at Cleo before running across the unsteady lotus and diving into the boiling water.

This is what he lived for! The daily fight with Apep especially as it calmed his desire to harm his brother, sisters and nephew like he had done in the past.

He broke the surface and quickly swam over to the mass of serpent muscle. The nails on his hands grew long, turning into claws he could use to grip on to the scales of the two fighting snakes. He grabbed on to one and the muscles twitched at the intrusion of the claws. Set gulped a breath as he went under as the snake he was on twisted.

As the bodies continued to twist, Apep and Horus taking turns to rear their heads up and squeeze their opponent's body, Set slowly made his way up Apep's body till he was at the neck.

Apep reared up and realised there was a god on his back and broke out of the fight with Horus to try to shake Set off. He twisted and turned. Set held on tight as again and again Apep dived under the water.

Apep rose high into the air, beginning to tire with Set now riding him like a bucking bronco. Set threw an arm out and shouted, "now!"

Cleo looked at the spear and then at Set, hesitating.

Set screamed, "now! I'll make sure you never make it out of here alive if you don't hurry up."

Cleo hefted the spear up as she had seen at the Olympics and films about ancient Greeks. Aiming it at Set she ran across the lotus and threw it toward him. She teetered on the edge but Sekhmet grabbed her by the belt and pulled her back before she fell in the water. Cleo landed on her bum panting, "thank you."

"You don't want to fall in the water."

They both watched the spear sail through the air, the papyrus rope trailing behind. Set caught the spear and with both hands on it slammed the point of the spear into Apep's neck. He grabbed the swinging rope and began to twist it around Apep's neck pulling it tighter and tighter. Apep's mouth was wide open but it was slammed shut by a coil of rope that Set lassoed around the demon's mouth. Apep tried to flex his muscles and weaken the rope but it only grew tighter instead. Set shouted, "call the barque and get Ra out of here."

The violently thrashing Apep caused huge ripples that broke the lotus from its stem. With the weight of the immortals and Cleo unevenly balanced the flower flipped over. Everyone was thrown into the water but they didn't land in water.

Cleo braced herself for hitting the water with no breath and having to kick back up to the surface. Instead she landed on the harder surface of compacted reeds that was the deck of Ra's barque. It left her feeling bruised and she just wanted to curl up and cry.

Reluctantly she stood up and was relieved to find she hadn't broken any bones. She looked around and found the barge was marooned on the reeded edge of a lake. Apep and Set were nowhere to be seen. The water was millpond still and so clear that when she looked over the side she saw a swirling current below the surface like it was another lake underneath them. She couldn't explain it but she had a feeling they had somehow fallen up to this deeper or shallower layer of the Egyptian netherworld. She had no idea how many times they had now descended or ascended.

Thoth came to stand beside her and looked out himself. Cleo glanced at the god and wondered if she dared ask where they were but decided the answer probably wouldn't make any sense. She was surprised to hear him ask, "are you hurt?"

"Err…"

"We have used you a lot. It hasn't affected you has it?"

"I don't know, I don't think so. I feel a bit bruised from the fall on to the barque."

"I'm not surprised."

"Have you not been hurt?"

Thoth shook his head and then remarked, "seems a fishing boat has capsized today."

Five bodies floated upside down with parts of their wooden boat and its contents scattered around them, a broken oar, a cool box and several plastic bottles of water. All of them were wearing t-shirts, shorts and trainers. A baseball cap floated upside down. It seemed even the modern day reached its long tendrils down here, even if it was just from those who drowned in the Nile.

"Those are modern bodies, from the time I'm from so you know time has moved on." Cleo observed.

Thoth commented, "they may not dress like us but they are currently lost kas who need to be reborn again so that they get a new opportunity to reach the Field of Reeds."

"And get stuck in that queue?" Cleo protested, "they are better off as lost souls

Beyond the wreckage and bodies there was a lone rock in the shape of a lotus flower balanced on a stone pillar stem. There was a swirl of water below it that hinted at something like an entrance to somewhere else.

From behind Thoth and Cleo came Isis, "where's Horus?! Where's my son?! Where's Set?"

Thoth looked around, "oh." He turned back to Cleo, "without Horus they will be unguided and not be led into the primeval waters where they will be reborn again."

There was a bloop sound close to the lotus rock. The still body of the flame patterned cobra bobbed to the surface and drifted to shore and got caught in the reeds. Isis let out a cry of dismay and jumped off the boat. She waded into the shadows and with Nephthys' help pulled the snake on to land where it shrank down into Horus' human form.

His body was limp and covered in black and purple bruises. As Isis pulled her son on to her lap she could feel all the broken bones. She began to cry and not silent tears. This was breast beating wailing that suggested she thought her son dead. Isis wanted to rub dirt on her skin and beat her breast as if she was a paid mourner in the wall paintings of a funerary procession. Nephthys knelt beside her sister and put her hand on Isis' shoulder, "he did it for you, to protect you."

Standing, looking down at the two sisters, Hathor

said with a roll of his eyes, "don't be so dramatic, he's not dead. With time he will heal."

Nephthys looked up and retorted, "he's needed now. Without him those kas will be cast adrift, never to find peace. They'll turn into demons and punish us and the mortals." She turned to Sekhmet, "you must heal him." Sekhmet shook her head.

Hathor said, with arms crossed, "well they should have been wearing life vests. See it as punishment."

Cleo's mouth dropped open at how callous Hathor was being especially as the ancient Egyptians hadn't even had life vests.

Sekhmet took a wary step closer to her sister for protection as she said, "I am tired. I have my own wounds to heal." She felt Hathor put a hand on her arm telling her to stay strong.

"Do it Sekhmet." Ra ordered from behind them all. Sekhmet scowled, "fine. Lie him down."

Isis hesitated. She looked at the two sisters, trying to work out if Sekhmet would obey or if they would do something else out of spite. Hathor had her arms crossed and snorted with distain while Sekhmet's shoulders had sunk. She felt sorry for Sekhmet as she did look tired and drained of energy. How much had Hathor claimed from her? And now Horus would be doing the same without him knowing it.

She lay her son on the ground and crossed his arms across his chest. She and Nephthys then stepped back to give Sekhmet space.

Sekhmet knelt beside Horus' prone body. From out of the air she produced a sistum and began to shake it over Horus' body as she held her other hand over his heart as she murmured spells.

No one spoke, no one moved as they watched Sekhmet working. They could all see her beginning to flag as she had said. Putting aside her material worries Isis knelt down opposite her and took hold of the lioness' hand. She began chanting the healing spells with Sekhmet. From her dress she pulled out an ankh amulet and placed it on Horus' chest.

The bruises began to fade and the bones knitted back together. Horus drew in a deep breath and slowly opened his eyes. The ankh was absorbed into his chest. Isis took a deep breath of relief herself and helped her son sit up.

Hathor caught her sister and wrapped protective arms around her as Sekhmet slumped. She glared at Isis for making her sister heal Horus. To her sister she murmured, "you are done. It's time for you to go home and rest." Sekhmet looked up into Hathor's concerned face, "you should too."

"Once I know Apep is secured again. Tomorrow we'll try and work out how he escaped."

"Yes, those tracks…" Sekhmet was already fading as she returned to her palace home. Hathor hoped Anubis would already have strolled through to take away her dead lion companions and left a litter of cubs in their place.

Horus leant on his mother and aunt as he got to tired feet. He glanced out to the water and took an unsteady step towards it. Isis grabbed her son's arm and held it so tight he winced at her fingernails digging into his skin. She said sternly, "no."

Emotionlessly he replied, "I have to."

"No, no, let them become demons. They chose to go out on the river without the right equipment." Isis protested. Horus sighed and carefully peeled his mother's fingers off his arm one by one. A red impression of her hand remained. He pushed and held his mother's arm in place by her side as he said firmly, "I must. We will have tomorrow night, and the night after, and the night after that."

"But that's tomorrow night." She protested, "the fact is I almost lost you tonight." She crossed her arms to stop herself reaching out for her son. She knew he was right and had a duty to perform but that didn't stop her from worrying.

He pointed behind her, "look, here come the lantern bearers to take you to the next hour."

Beyond Ra's defined edge of light was pitch blackness but now in it were four dots of moving light. As they came closer the four circles of light became four flickering oil lamps being carried by four veiled goddesses, heads bowed so their faces couldn't be seen. Their translucent dresses glowed with an ethereal light which lingered on their footprints.

In silence they came to a stop and spread out into a line, their footsteps fading behind them. One softly spoke, "come with us."

Ra turned to the group, "it is time to move on."

Cleo was the last of the group to follow the lamp bearers. She was watching Horus cross the lake to the drowned. She was pleased Horus was willing to do his duty to the dead unlike the rest of them.

He walked on the surface, each bare footed step causing a ripple. Stepping on to the stone lotus it began to close into a bud just as a real one does in the late evening across the living world. Horus stood at the bud's tip and with a long staff began to stir up the water where the swirl of current was. The swirling grew faster and then began to form into a whirlpool that span downwards to the lake within a lake, spiraling round the stem of the lotus.

The whirlpool began pulling in the bodies and the fishing party's debris. The bodies slipped down easily while Horus watched on, a grim expression on his face and leaning on his staff. The debris got spat out, returning to the surface close to the lake's shore. As the last body was caught by the whirlpool Horus held up a hand to acknowledge Cleo witnessing the act that sent the drowned straight to Nun and her primeval waters.

Cleo slowly turned away and realised she was soon to be left behind if she didn't catch up quickly. She began to jog after them. Thoth glanced back and slowed at hearing her footsteps.

HOUR 11

They entered a new space where an empty throne was on a dais. A shield of wood rested against the chair. It had been oiled till it shone apart from where a join had been patched from some violent blow. Behind the throne were six pits with flickering flames. A serpent demon lay close by, guarding them.

Hearing movement behind her Cleo turned. There was a shout down the tunnel, "either help me or get out of my way!"
Cleo bumped into Thoth as she moved out of the way.

Set dragged Apep into the chamber. He had a big grin on his face. Once again he had defeated Ra's enemy and Horus, his nephew, had failed. The fact his sisters weren't red eyed from weeping told him that sadly his nephew hadn't died. There would always be next time.

Normally he just guarded the demon who could bring the world to a chaotic end but every once in a while it was good to let the demon free and see what havoc it could cause. It was fortunate how it had been perfectly timed with the appearance of the dumb female khat. He looked at her now, staring wide eyed at Apep's body and had to guess it was luck that had kept her alive.

He returned to his own thoughts and noted the missing Sekhmet. He had to hope that his purposely confusing tracks wouldn't be traceable back to him, although… He smiled to himself, it would be nice to have them remember he was just as powerful as his siblings, just forced to live in their shadows.

Apep's body twitched and there was a growl from the edge of the space, "not here you don't."
Neith stalked in and kicked the serpent who flinched away from her foot. She wore a breastplate of leather strips over her dress and on her head was the red crown of Lower Egyp. Everyone except Ra and Set dropped to their knees, Thoth pulling Cleo down with him and kowtowed to the ancient goddess. She didn't acknowledge their presence, her eyes were on the rope wrapped Apep and Set.

Apep rolled his eyes and grimaced as he tried to stretch the rope round his mouth and neck. Set grinned at the ancient goddess as she remarked, "good job."
He pretended he didn't see the frown of suspicion that flickered across her face. He knew she would suspect him as she saw a lot more than the others. His smile which became a smirk. She chose to ignore it and turned to her son Ra.

Ra bowed his head as his mother advanced. She held her hands out, "I'm glad to see you well."
He didn't move as he stiffly replied, "mother."

"Always so awkward with me." She sighed and pursed her lips. More brightly she added, "I see you have someone who doesn't belong here."

"Yes and hopefully she will return from where she came as I rise as the sun."

"Let's hope so otherwise there are entities down here who will take advantage." She strolled over to where Cleo knelt and lifted her head with a sandalled foot to study her.
Cleo slowly looked up as Neith asked, "do you know who I am?"

"I…"

"You haven't heard of me have you?" There was a flash of anger in her eyes and Cleo quickly looked at the ground.

"Mother." Ra said with a warning tone, "don't torment her. It's not her fault she ended up here and doesn't know who you are.”

“Have none of you been teaching her?”

“She’s not staying long enough to need to know. Preferably it would be best she forgot all of this.” Thoth said.

“I am stuck down here with nothing to do, half remembered by a select few if at all these days and every night you all visit but it’s only fleeting. Give the girl to me as company.”

“No. She doesn’t belong here. Now open the path so I can be reborn.” Ra interrupted. He was used to her grumblings. He never knew who was worse, Amun who didn’t care even with all the temples, shrines and offerings dedicated to him, or Neith, a grumpy goddess who didn’t think she ever got her due.

Neith glowered down at Cleo, “hmpfh.” She crossed her arms, turned on her heel and marched over to her throne. She sat down on it and glared at her creation. She couldn’t call him son since she and Amun had never actually copulated. They had discussed the creation of Ra and something to balance him and that had become Apep. Perhaps she and Amun had been foolish in their creation of Apep but it was too late now. At least Ra was reminded every night that he wasn’t all powerful, even if he rolled the sun through the sky every day.

Hopefully Set had ensured there would be no trace back to her and himself. She was a little disappointed that Ra didn’t look any worse than normal. Apep would received his punishment for failure as normal. She ordered, “dispose of Apep and then I’ll open your path through.”

“Khat, come here.” Set ordered.

“I do have a name you know.” Cleo retorted.

“Whatever. Just come here.” Set knew none of the others would help him.

Cleo slowly got to her feet, glanced at the ancient goddess

on her throne, and then at Set whose sandalled foot was now on Apep's head.

"This lot are too wimpish to help." He smirked, "so you get to help me. You and I get to dismember this foolish demon and ensure he doesn't rise till the new night."
Ra nodded his approval at Set's words. Hathor scowled, she was no wimp but she had to be ready to protect her father if Apep escaped while being dismembered.

"You will start at the tail and I will be at the head." Set ordered.

"Why me?" Cleo demanded, "Thoth is probably stronger than me. I'm sure Hathor would happily show you her skills, test them against yours."

"Because you are a nobody." Set sneered, "you are nothing more than a shabti so I'll put you to use. Come here and take this." He held out a wooden handled flint axe, "start hacking."
Cleo could feel Apep's eyes on her, glaring at her as she took the axe and was glad to be at the tail end.

She lifted the axe above her head, braced herself and brought it down as if she was chopping wood which she had never done either. It went into the flesh but stopped when it hit the bone.

She pulled on the axe and staggered backwards once the flesh released the axe, blood splattering on her legs and her dress. She grimaced and was relieved the blood wasn't acidic like James Cameron's Aliens' drool. She lifted the axe again and again, bringing it down again and again. Soon she was covered in blood and the tip of the tail was separated from the body. She stepped back breathing heavily, axe hanging down heavy in her hand as a stone shabti appeared and dragged the piece of Apep's body away to one of the pits where the flesh hissed and spat in the heat of the flames.

At the head Set bowed to Apep and murmured a

spell that insured Apep would be reborn once Ra had risen into the sky. Then he raised his spear into the air and it became an axe. His axe cut straight through Apep's flesh and bone with one whack. There was a high pitched scream as the head was separated from the body.

Two gold shabtis stepped from behind the throne and lifted Apep's head from the ground. They took it to the pits where it was unceremoniously thrown in.

By the time all of Apep's body was in the pits the fires within them raged and the cavern had grown hot. Black smoke billowed out from the pits as well as the stench of burning flesh. Cleo had to wipe sweat from her forehead with the back of her hand, smearing blood as she did. She didn't dare look down at her clothes. She wanted a long warm shower to wash Apep's blood and the smell of his flesh off her.

The snake that lay guarding the pits had grown more bloated with every piece thrown into the pit as if it was being fed at the same time. Now it had slithered off to digest it all and Apep's ba would find its way to the body to be reborn.

Set sat down on the edge of the dais and accepted the drink offered him by a shabti. He gestured over to Cleo, "she deserves one too."
Neith reached down and rubbed his head and like a dog being stroked by his owner he leant into the hand and smiled. If he had had a tail it would have been wagging. For the moment he was her favourite.

Ra stepped up to the bottom of Neith's dais and gestured for Isis and Nephthys to step forward with him. Thoth joined Cleo and murmured, "time to woo her."

"What is he going to do?" Cleo asked back, hoping he wasn't going to offer her. Did Egyptians ever do human sacrifices?!

They watched as Ra dropped down on to one knee. Behind him the sister goddesses approached, each holding a crown. One held the red crown of Lower Egypt while the other had the long conical white crown of Upper Egypt. As the sisters bowed their heads and offered the crowns with outstretched arms, he said, "oh noble lady of creation and opener of pathways, please accept these gifts as recognition of your guardianship over all the lands. You are there at my birth and there at my death and that I am grateful for."

"Hmpfh." Neith waved the two crowns away and off to one side a path revealed itself, lit by a solitary starshaped light.

Thoth whispered to Cleo, "Tioumoutiri, the morning star. Now we can see about getting you home."

"Where or what is home?" Cleo challenged, "I don't know if this is all real or whether I have been dreaming or maybe I knocked myself unconscious so this is something else, I don't know the name of."

He looked thoughtful, "I don't know either. We'll just have to see what happens."

"And what will happen?"

"I think you should go through the Hall of Two Truths. Osiris can ensure you are sent to the right place. They will all know you don't belong here. Have you enjoyed yourself?"

"Not particularly."

Thoth chuckled, "your kings find that as well. They are in such awe of Ra they don't even realise what is happening to them."

"Will I remember any of this?"

Thoth shrugged and then said, "come on, before we are stuck here keeping Neith amused and she is hard to entertain." He pulled a face which made Cleo giggle.

She hurried after Thoth as he strode towards the opening.

HOUR 12

There was a hum which rose in volume as they stepped out of the corridor and on to the deck of the lunar barque. They were in a cavern with a warm pink hue to it as if the sun was on the verge of rising above the horizon. The sides of the cavern moved as if they were inside a breathing body. On the banks of the underworld's version of the Nile were lots of akhs singing their hearts out in joy that Ra had survived another night. Standing on the deck was Shu who smiled, "you have survived another night then?"

"Only just." Hathor remarked grimly, "there were casualties."

"I'm sure, but you are all here now. Ready to light the world again?"

"Of course." Ra said.

Cleo sensed a shadow and looked up. Floating high above them was the solar barque with Ma'at waving, a bandage round her neck where Cleo had stabbed her with the spear. The feather tucked into her headband wafted in a gentle breeze and bounced as her body moved in her excitement at seeing the others.

Cleo's attention was fixated on the ethereal Ma'at and she didn't realise at first that Ra was standing in front of her, studying her, until he cleared his throat. She blinked and looked startled to find him so close, "s..sorry."
He smiled softly at her, "this is where our association comes to an end."

"Oh."

"It is time for me to be reborn."

"And me? How do I leave here?"

"You go to the Hall of Two Truths."

"But I'm not dead." Cleo protested.

"I am the sun. Osiris looks after the underworld."

"I can't be stuck here. I can't be dead!" She wailed as the realisation sank in that she might actually be dead. Had she really hit her head that hard when she tripped? She put a hand to her head and felt all over but couldn't feel any open wounds or sticky patches of blood in her hair.

He cocked his head, "you are not dead but only Osiris can send you back to the living world."

"Then why bring me on this journey? You could have left me all the way back at the beginning with Osiris."

"It was safer to keep you with us."

"Safer?!" She exclaimed, "was I really safe being made to climb a rope in a high wind, being made to pin a giant snake to the ground, going over a waterfall?"

He blinked.

"Is that all you've got?! You are meant to be the all powerful Ra. Send me back." She felt frustrated by the god who wasn't behaving like a god should in her opinion.

"No." He said with warning.

"Am I going to be weighed?" She changed tactic. She needed all the information she could get to survive and be sent home. She knew the basics of the ceremony but she didn't have the advantage of the spells and amulets and knowledge that the ancient Egyptians had.

He shrugged, "that is up to him." He straightened and he grew taller before Cleo's eyes.

She took a step backwards and had to shade her eyes to look at him. Oblivious to Cleo's emotions he smiled, "thank you. You have helped more than you'll ever realise."

She chose not to say anything, that she thought differently. She had veered from being an unwanted witness to the unfolding events of the night to a reluctant assistant in it all and had felt like nothing more than a slave to their demands.

"Now, Thoth, can you…"

"Of course." Thoth put his hand on Cleo's shoulder, "this way."

"Do I not…?" The questioned fell silent, unfinished, as Thoth guided her off the barque.

"We can't let you into all of our secrets." Thoth chuckled.

Back in the passageway Thoth pressed a hand on the wall and a door silently opened. A goddess stood on the other side to take Cleo back to the queue. Thoth pushed Cleo through. The goddess murmured, "can you remember where you were?"

Cleo spun round to ask Thoth but she found herself looking at a blank wall. She spun back to the goddess, "what about all the kas waiting? I can't be stuck in that line for eternity?!"

She turned back to the wall and hit it with her fists and with the flat of her feet until they hurt, "don't you dare leave me here!"

"Stop you're whining and get in line." A ka exclaimed, "be glad you survived whatever was behind that door, that your kin gave you an amulet or the spell."

She turned to the ka and saw the line stretching in both directions and felt like she was back to the beginning. She protested, "I don't belong here, I'm not dead."

"I think you are. You wouldn't be here if you were still alive."

"I have to have just banged my head."

"Come my child." The goddess took Cleo's hand and led her down the line.

Cleo couldn't find the energy to resist. Tears formed in her eyes and she tried to blink them away.

On the other side of the wall, back in Nut's belly, the goddesses and Set bowed as Ra passed them as he approached Shu.

As if he was a child being held up by a parent Ra was lifted skyward by Shu, up to Ma'at's hands which were reaching down. With a brief scrabble of sandalled feet on the boat and Ma'at pulling him he eventually tumbled into the boat, his dignity not intact as he swore when he landed hard on the deck. Ma'at covered her mouth to hide the giggle. Ra gave her a glare as he stood and brushed off a few reed fibres off his linen kilt. She remarked, "give me a break. That poor soul that you dragged along with you did injury me."
Normally she would have been able to swing him up so he leapt over the side of the solar barque.
"What else was I supposed to do? She was out of place." He retorted.

"And she still is." Ma'at calmly replied.

"She's Osiris' problem now."

"Along with all those other kas waiting and waiting. You are his father, tell him to open the court again. It has been too long."

"I could point out you haven't done much to encourage him either."

"The world is out of balance. I have been trying and failing." Her bottom lip began to tremble.

She was trying so hard but the world had changed, those who were worshipped had changed and not enough worried about the fact the world wasn't in balance like the ancient Egyptians. The world had expanded beyond the borders of Egypt and Kush starting with the Greeks and Romans. When only Egypt knew of her, she had control but she couldn't balance the whole world.

She was aware of the long line of kas that needed

their hearts to be weighed and there were even some that were closer to Cleo's time than her's, dressed in huge dresses enclosed up to their necks. She had walked amongst them, invisible to them and had stared at those that were unusually dressed and couldn't understand how they coped with the wide skirts and long sleeves in the heat of Egypt. They, even now, still had a look of excitement in their faces as they whispered to each other and clicked their fingers for the attention of a shabti and demanded tea or coffee and the shabti always managed to produce what they needed including a small table and chairs for them to sit on.

She would have to check on the girl the next time she walked through. She hoped Cleo would be freed eventually like all the rest.

She turned her attention back to the present and bowed her head to Ra, "now I am done, have a nice day." She walked across to the prow and sat on the raised edge before slipping off to be caught by Thoth. She happily snuggled into his chest as he held her off the ground cradled in his arms.

He kissed the top of her head and held her tight. He didn't like to see her suffering and he knew she was, and not just at this moment. The whole world and not just Egypt was out of sorts and poor Ma'at couldn't cope.

Above them Ra settled in the solar barque's cabin as it began moving. Behind it a large scarab beetle slowly pushed it towards a large glowing red spot high on the side of the cavern.

In a blaze of golden light Ra broke out of the underworld and between Nut's thighs. To anyone awake early enough to see the sun rise her thighs looked like clouds stained red by the rising sun. There was a loud moan that only Ra heard as the boat pushed through Nut's vagina.

HOUR: WHO KNOWS!

Cleo sat on the floor of the corridor, back against the wall, head buried in her arms that rested on her knees. A foot pushed the dusting of sand around like a nervous twitch. She had no idea how long she had been waiting. It could have been hours, it could have been months, and still she didn't know if she was dead or alive or unconscious, her body waiting for her ba to come back to wake it like Ra's.

The kas either side of her ignored her. At first they had protested at her being slotted in between them and complained that she was queue jumping. They also protested at the state and smell of her. They demanded the shabatis bring Cleo water to wash with. That had yet to happen.

She looked up briefly as the line shuffled forward a couple of centimetres and then stopped again. Cleo didn't bother moving. What was the point? She would never reach the front and she had no amulets and didn't know any of the spells to get through doors or to fend off any demons.

Nephthys walked down the long line, invisible to everyone in it. She may have been disdainful towards Cleo the night the khat had been with them but she knew Cleo had spoken some truths. The kas had been waiting a long time, a long, long time. The line hadn't shrunk much over time either, just grown larger, even with a few being picked off.

She paused as she came to Cleo and pursed her lips as she thought about the misplaced khat. She'd never seen anyone look so forlorn while waiting for their turn. The khat had no amulets or scraps of papyrus with spells so probably wouldn't even make it to the Hall of Two Truths.

She revealed herself making the nervous kas flatten themselves against the walls in awe. The surrounding kas fell silent as those further ahead or behind peered up and down out of curiosity, whispering to each other. This was the most excitement they had had in a long time. Ignoring the kas Nephthys crouched down and put a hand on Cleo's head, "come child."

Cleo slowly lifted her head to see who was speaking to her. She grew wary at seeing it was Nephthys. She found herself saying with a bitter tone, "what do you want?"

"You don't belong here."

"I know that. I told you all that. They know that." Cleo gestured at the surrounding kas, "yet you shoved me in this line to wait an eternity like everyone else here. They don't deserve to be here either. They'll have loved ones who are waiting to see them in the Field of Reeds."

"You are right but I'm here for you."

"You going to give me to Ammit?" Cleo challenged with the same bitter tone.

Nephthys stood up and with an authoritative voice said, "Cleopatra Philips you are coming with me. Your heart will be weighed."

"Does that mean I am dead?" Cleo whispered; fear having contracted her throat.

Nephthys held out a hand, "you can stay here if you want."

"I'll take her place." One of the kas said and others began to say the same, hands waving to get Nephthys' attention. They began to push forward and crowd Cleo out.

Cleo realised her opportunity was rapidly disappearing and got up and reached for the offered hand.

Nephthys grabbed hold of it and pulled her through the group that was becoming agitated. With an arm round Cleo the goddess turned on the crowd and snapped, "enough!" The kas fell silent and bowed their heads at being chastised by the goddess.

The quiet didn't last. As if fired up by Cleo's words first there was the shuffling of feet then nudging as they all tried to persuade each other to become spokesperson. One was pushed forward. He glanced back with a look of panic but was shooed forward. Reluctantly the ka turned back to face Nephthys. He dropped to his knees, hands clasped together, "noble goddess. We ask that you speak to the Lord Osiris. We all have relatives and friends we want to be reunited with, some could even be in this line with us and we wouldn't know it. We want to receive Ra's blessing every night and feel his light warm us. We have all been here too long."

"I will speak with him but now you must let me through." Nephthys stood straight backed, dominating the space. The kas shuffled back and let the goddess and Cleo through.

Cleo found herself once again at the huge false door. The guard at the door, still wearing his Stargate like helmet rolled his eyes, "not you again. Do you know how long it took me to calm the line down?"

"Enough." Nephthys decreed, "open the door and let us through."

"And them?" He jerked his spear at the kas looking on with agitated curiosity.

"They won't do anything."

"Are you sure?" He eyed them warily.

"Yes. Now open the door." To reassure him the goddess glared at the kas and said, "behave yourselves or I'll find a

demon you don't have a spell for."
The kas took a step back, some clinging to each other and glancing nervously at black openings they had survived next to for so long.
Nephthys turned back to the guard, "happy now?"

"Thank you." He put a hand behind his back and pressed a hidden button on the false door so with a creak it popped open and Cleo could see the split down the middle that indicated two doors.
Nephthys gestured to the doors, "in you go."

Cleo didn't hesitate for long. She pushed the door open enough so that she could slip through only to come up against two spear wielding goddesses, their spears crossed so she couldn't see beyond them. They looked Cleo over and then sniffed as one said, "who prepared this body?"

"Why has she even been let through? I thought no one was being let through."

"Umm, excuse me, but *she* is standing here." Cleo crossed her arms, "I know I stink and I know I am covered in Apep's blood. I just want to go home."

"You have fought with Apep? You protected Ra?" There was awe in the voice of the lefthand guard.
Cleo pulled herself up to make herself look taller. She jutted out her chin, "yes."

"Well, we can't have you presenting yourself to the Lord Osiris looking like that. Where is Qebhet?" The guard let out a piercing whistle and a shabti shuffled into view. She ordered, "go find Qebhet and make sure she brings warm water and a washcloth."
The shabti stiffly bowed its head and shuffled off.
The goddess guard turned back to Cleo, "there we go. Now, did you really see Apep? Did you fight him?"
Not sure where this conversation was going to go Cleo carefully said, "yes."

She was relieved to see Qebhet appear. The goddess

had a jackal head but there was a suggestion of the feminine with a hoop ear ring in one of her ears along with the fine sheaf dress. She carried a linen cloth folded over one arm and large dish of warm water in her hands. She bowed her head towards Cleo and her voice was like water flowing from fountains, soft and twinkly, as she said, "I apologise that no one came to get me sooner. Please, here is water to clean yourself."

Cleo watched the water turn pink as she wrung the cloth over the bowl. She had had to rub hard at all the dried on blood on her skin. There was nothing she could do about the clothes. She used damp hands to try and tidy her hair. She turned to the guard with a tentative smile, "thank you. How do I look?"

"Not perfect but better. You may now proceed."

The spears separated and the guards made room for Cleo. She stepped up so she stood between them, in the large doorway that led to the next room. She took a deep breath. She was on her own now, truly on her own.

The room seemed to stretch for miles, with a pillared colonnade to guide everyone to the stage. On either side of the colonnade were the forty-two divine gods wrapped up in shrouds looking more like Incan mummies than Egyptian ones. Looking at them she had no idea what any of their names were and she feared being eaten before she could even petition Osiris.

Slowly she walked up the colonnade. She could hear the judges whispering. Looking over she saw them leaning into their neighbours and murmuring behind hands hidden in their shrouds. She turned away and focused on the stage ahead of her.

Lying in front of the stage was Ammit, the demoness who would eat any heart that failed the weighing. Her hindquarters were that of a hippo. The front half was the dusty yellow chest and large paws of a lion. Her head was a crocodile with blood stained teeth. She lifted her head from her paws and weakly growled before lowering her head. She was hungry and hadn't eaten in a long time.

On the stage was Osiris on his throne with Thoth as a baboon at his feet with his scribe palette and board on his crossed legs to record the results. Thoth smiled warmly at Cleo, hoping it would give her confidence. In the centre of the stage were the scales used to weigh the heart against Ma'at's ostrich sized Feather of Truth which Ma'at currently held, stroking it as she sat on the edge of the stage, legs dangling and swinging. Ma'at looked up and beamed at Cleo as if she was a young woman, not an ancient goddess. On the other side of the scales stood Anubis holding a small box.

Osiris remarked from his throne, "so you have made it here."

"Only because Nephthys brought me here. What about everyone else? They have been waiting patiently for centuries."

"For many of them their names are lost to time. No one remembers them and they don't remember their own names." Osiris stood and crossed the stage to look down at Cleo.

"They don't know that." She took a step back, cowered by his regal bearing. He dominated the space. She wondered if he didn't like being challenged.

"And they don't need to." He warned her.

"I could try and find their names."

"Their names are lost, don't even try. I feel sorry for them but there is nothing I can do. Enough of them. You are here for a reason. Do you know what that is?"

"I'm hoping you are going to send me home."

"And I hope I can as well."

"I don't know the names of the judges."

"I think I can forgive you that. What is your name?"

"Cleopatra Philips." She stood straighter as if she was back at school in front of the headmaster.

"And do you think you have been a good person?"

She reflected on her mistakes, many she had not told anyone of, the stolen sweets from the pick and mix, using the last of a housemate's fancy shower gel, stealing money out of her mum's purse, pushing a friend on the playground and not saying sorry. She was sure there were more serious wrongs but she could only think of the little things as over time they would add up. She finally said, "I hope so."

"Then let the weighing of the heart begin." Osiris announced loud enough for everyone to hear and retreated to his throne.

Anubis opened the box he held and lifted out Cleo's heart. She felt her chest constrict as if Anubis had pulled it from her body. She put a hand to where her heart would be and could feel it beating behind her ribs. She looked up at Anubis wide eyed and he smiled knowingly at her.

The heart dropped the scales but the feather hadn't been put on yet. Her eyes didn't move from the scales as the feather was placed on the other plate. She held her breath as the scales shifted up and down.

It was the longest two minutes of her life as the scales shifted up and down until they balanced. The room was silent as Osiris made a decision. The scales shifted one last time and the feather dipped lower than her heart. Cleo released her breath. She had made it… Just.

Osiris gave a faint nod Cleo only just saw. The god nudged Thoth with his foot.

Anubis remarked without emotion, "you are free to go and enjoy the Wernes akh."

"Am I dead then?"

Osiris' mouth twitched, "you'll have to see."

Cleo looked to Thoth. All he did was raise an eyebrow.

Cleo had to bite her tongue. She was feeling angry with all of them, at Thoth for basically abandoning her, at Osiris who was being so cryptic. She wasn't going to be getting a straight answer from any of them. They had fallen back into their mysterious roles. She remarked, with frustration, "I suppose I should say thank you."
Osiris waved the gratitude away as Anubis pointed to a door hidden in the corner or had it only now been revealed as Cleo had passed the test.

Cleo ran, pausing long enough to hug Ma'at who giggled at the embrace. She didn't know where she would find herself but one thing for certain she wanted a large coffee and to lie in the sun and feel Ra's rays warming her skin. That was probably what she had missed the most, the warmth of the sun.

She didn't pause at the doorway, didn't hesitate, just ran through it…..

…… She blinked and found herself in a low-lit room. Slowly she turned her head to see someone sitting next to her, head hanging down as if asleep, hands clasped together. As her brain started to wake up she realised the person wasn't dressed in modern clothes. She began to pay attention to the room. It was painted with a scene of reeds and birds all the way round the room. The bed she lay on had a thin straw mattress but the blanket was soft linen. There was a footboard but no headboard and her head was higher than her feet. She sat up and shouted, "Fuck you Ra!"
The woman beside her startled awake.

The Egyptian pantheon is an interesting one. As the kingdom grew and finally combined together from Upper and Lower Egypt the gods from the absorbed regions were added to the pantheon then they began to merge. For example Amen and Ra were considered separate entities and the same person at various stages. Orisis and Sokar are the same and Sekhmet is considered the aggressive side of Hathor. I have chosen to treat them as separate entities as they are mentioned separately in the hours of night. Following this little author note is a list of all the gods mentioned and a bit more about each.

The Book of Gates has been translated and interpreted several times with my main resources being The Book of Gates by E.A.Wallis Budge where he discusses the translation from the version of the Book of Gates that was found in the tomb of Seti I. I also used the Book of Myths and Legends of Ancient Egypt by Joyce Tyldesley and the interpretation of the Book of Gates by Andreas Schweizer under the title of 'The Sungod's Journey through the Netherworld'. I have followed along in that vein using them to help me build the journey through the underworld and then creating my own fictional interpretation which as I wrote the first version found it becoming more surreal in the vein of Monty Python. My rewrite I built on that.

<h1 style="text-align:center">List of Gods</h1>

Aker- An ancient god of earth and the horizon. He guarded the eastern and western borders of the netherworld and was often portrayed as two lions facing away from each other with the sun resting on their backs.

Anubis- Jackal headed God of the underworld and mummification. The original lord of the Dead until Osiris took that position during the Middle Kingdom. He resides as steward over the Weighing of the heart.

Amun- Also known as Amon, Amen and Amun-Ra. He was the chief deity of the New Kingdom and patron deity of Thebes. He was seen as a creator god, solar god and fertility god.

Amentet- wife and/or female version of Amun. She was thought to have been there before the creation of Ra with Amun.

Ammet- demoness/goddess with the forequarters of a lion, hindquarters of a hippo and the head of a crocodile. Consumed any impure hearts in the Hall of Truth.

Apep- the embodiment of chaos. Has been considered Ra's brother or even born of him as a balance to Ra's light.

Geb- ancient god of earth, born of Ra. Father of Osiris, Isis, Nephthys and Set.

Hathor- The Eye of Ra. She acted as protector for Ra as he travelled through the netherworld. She was considered a protector of women, a goddess of love, fertility, pleasure and music. She could also be angered where she could become Sekhmet.

Horus- Falcon headed son of Osiris and Isis. God of kingship and the sky where his eyes were considered to be the morning and evening star.

Isis- A powerful goddess and enchantress and healer. Wife to Osiris and mother of Horus.

Ma'at- The personification of truth, justice, harmony and balance. It is her feather that is used to measure the ka's heart and determine who is allowed through to paradise.

Neith- another ancient goddess of war and creation. Another contender for mother of Ra.

Nephthys- goddess of air and family. Sister of isis and wife of Set.

Nun- another name for the primeval waters where Ra emerged from.

Nut- goddess of the sky and heavens. Wife of Geb.

Osiris- was originally king of the mortal realm till he is killed by his brother Set where he becomes god/king of the underworld and resides over many courts in the afterlife including the Weighing of the Heart.

Ra- The sun god who is either ram headed, falcon headed or a scarab beetle. He travels through the sky during the day bringing light to the masses and during the night bringing light to the underworld while also being reborn and fighting off Apep with the assistances of the other gods.

Sekhmet- lioness headed goddess of war and considered

one of the options for the Eye of Ra. The angry version of Hathor.

Set- God of war and chaos. Brother/husband to Nephthys. He also guards Apep in the netherworld.

Shu- God of air. He is forced to separate his daughter Nut and son Geb to ensure that people can populate the world.

Sokar- One of the Gods of the Dead who gets merged with Osiris in later years. A patron to tomb builders and mummification.

Tefnut- goddess of rainfall and sister to Shu.

Tem- an older, predynastic version of Atum.

Thoth- god of science, messengers and scribes. Ra's right hand man and sorts out Ra's problems and records the results from the weighing of the heart.

Thank you

If you have got this far, as an independent author I would like to say thank you for purchasing this book and I hope you have enjoyed it. With no support from a big publishing house every purchase and review mean something to me so please spread the word and write a review. You can find me on Instagram as @f_garstang_author and let me know personally what you thought. You'll also see what I am working on and what will be coming out.

I am a multi genre author and I also have the below out:

Historical: The Crusade's Secrets
Historical Fantasy: Kukulcan's Messenger
Historical Romance: Masked
Historical Supernatural: The Dacha in the Forest
Fantasy Series: The Defenders of the Valley
                 The Lost God
                 The Daughters of Scyth.
                 The Basilisk's Revenge
Romance: Biker Leather and Woolly Sheep.

www.ingramcontent.com/pod-product-compliance
Lightning Source LLC
Chambersburg PA
CBHW061221210726
48294CB00006B/1924